D0615373

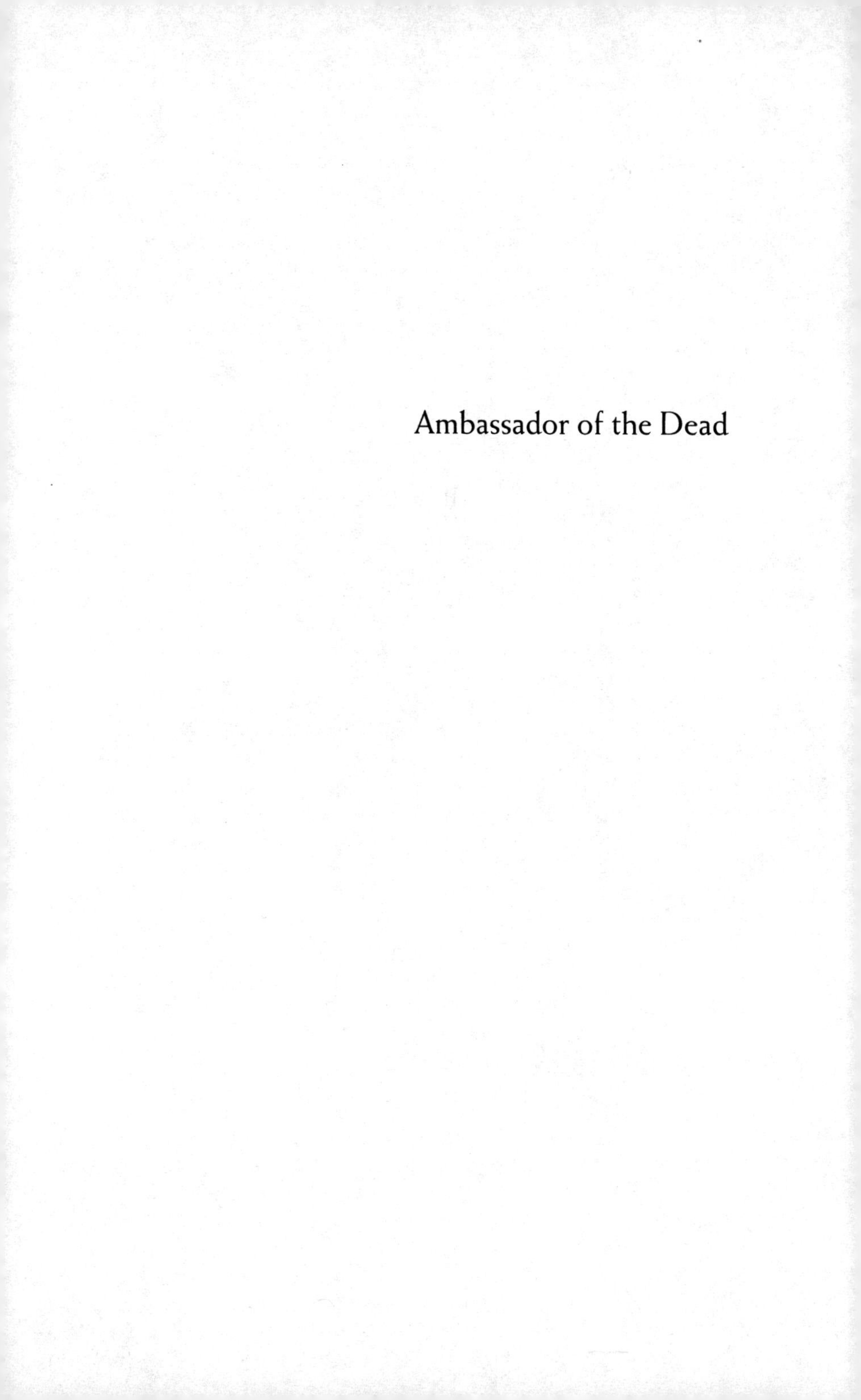

Ambassador of the Dead

ALSO BY ASKOLD MELNYCZUK

What Is Told

Ambassador of the Dead

a novel

Askold Melnyczuk

COUNTERPOINT PRESS WASHINGTON, D.C.

This book is a work of fiction. Names, characters, places, and incidents either are products of the author's imagination or are used fictitiously. Any resemblance to actual events or persons, living or dead, is entirely coincidental.

Parts of this novel first appeared in *The Antioch Review, The Southwest Review*, and *Story Quarterly*. My thanks to the journals' editors—Robert Fogarty, Willard Spiegelman, and M.M.M. Hayes respectively—for their support.

Thanks also to the Massachusetts Cultural Council and to the Lila Wallace Readers' Digest Foundations; to my friends, for their encouragement; to my editor, Dawn Seferian; and especially to my agent, Lane Zachary.

Library of Congress Cataloging-in-Publication Data
Melnyczuk, Askold.
Ambassador of the dead / Askold Melnyczuk.
p. cm.
ISBN 1-58243-132-9 (alk. Paper)
1. Ukrainian Americans—Fiction. 2. Mothers and sons—Fiction.
3. Male friendship—Fiction. 4. New Jersey—Fiction.
5. Physicians—Fiction. I. Title.
PS3563.E445 A8 2001
813'.54—dc21 00-065864

Book design and composition by Mark McGarry, Texas Type & Book Works
Set in Weiss

COUNTERPOINT
P.O. Box 65793, Washington, D.C. 20035–5793
Counterpoint is a member of the Perseus Books Group

10 9 8 7 6 5 4 3 2 1

for Alex

CONTENTS

A Family of Kruks 1

The Disappearing Sickness 37

The Ambassador of the Dead 107

The Woman Who Defeated Stalin 191

The Invisible World 253

Nothing remains in its proper place. Everything is somewhere else. But a being that is not in its proper place is in exile, in need of being led back and redeemed. The breaking of the vessels continues into all the further stages of emanation and creation: everything is in some way broken, everything has a flaw, everything is unfinished.

GERSHOM SCHOLEM

And what the dead had no speech for, when living,
They can tell you, being dead: the communication
Of the dead is tongued with fire beyond the language of the living.

T. S. ELIOT

A Family of Kruks

1

Ada Kruk was sitting in near darkness when I entered the living room. Everything around her, what I could see of it, appeared neat and in its place—magazines and books rose in dusty piles on the coffee and end tables. Embroidered curtains muted the late light, lending the apartment the stillness of a museum after closing hour.

I put down my bag, took off my coat and folded it across my arm, scattering snow onto the carpet. It was cold. The place had tall windows loose in their casements. Stiff from the flight, I rubbed my neck and cleared my throat, already tingling. I felt watched by faded wallpaper showing horsemen riding to hounds in pursuit, presumably, of a fox. The pattern couldn't have been less suitable for the apartment, the third floor of a triple-decker, and the neighborhood, the port section of a city in northern New Jersey, where I was born thirty-some years earlier, and which was now dominated by Haitians. Yet the fact was Ada tacked that paper up herself, in a bad moment, to honor her passion for Anton, an émigré poet. In this world, you have to be nuts to love a poet.

Ada, whose long, even-featured face seemed stretched by the earrings dangling down almost to her shoulders, sat motionless as one of those mechanical fortune tellers under glass you used to see at carnivals. *Donna* Kruk, I wanted to say.

"You've gained weight," she greeted me.

"Should I turn on the light?"

"Why? I know what you look like. We both know what's in this room. It hasn't changed much since you were here last."

A confusion fell over me in which I seemed to forget myself. Instead of treating Ada like any other would-be patient, I felt obliged to obey her, just as I had when I was boy.

"Will you excuse me?" she said, looking past me.

I watched her rise from her armchair and move laboriously down the hall, groping the furniture and walls for support. Her long black dress now hid the ankles she'd once flaunted. Soon she would require a cane. As I marked the slurs of time, her brother Viktor slunk timidly in to ask if I wanted something to drink. He was clutching a glass of clear liquid I assumed was vodka. The cigarette between his spongy lips chuffed smoke. In the bad light, his face was the color of a faded coffee stain.

"Thanks, no. Why did she call me?"

The phone rang that morning at my home in Boston where, as usual on Sundays, my wife and I were in bed with the paper. I let my machine screen the call. When the voice identified itself as Ada, the mother of my boyhood friend Alex, I picked up the receiver. My heart tightened—why would she, who'd never called, call me now? I hadn't seen her since our conversation after my father's funeral. She must have gotten my number from Alex.

Her voice sounded grave. She asked whether I was still a doctor—as if it were a thing from which one resigned. I nodded into the receiver: What did she need? Was it an emergency? It was. Why not call a local physician? Couldn't do that. She needed me to come to Roosevelt. Right away. She couldn't say why. She'd explain everything as soon as I arrived. I doubt Ada ever visited Boston—in her mind, I was practically next door.

I found it impossible to refuse her. Since my parents' deaths, I've all but lost touch with the community in which I'd been raised. This might have been a final chance to reconnect, though Ada made for a pretty shakey bridge. I gave Shelley the short version—she'd heard me mention both Ada and Alex many times over the years but had never actually met them—and by noon I was at Logan on standby for the next Delta Shuttle. In fact, Alex had called me a few days earlier for the first time in many months. He hadn't sounded well, but then he hadn't sounded well in ages. We spoke briefly—he updated me on problems at work, I told him about a lawsuit a patient was threatening—and we promised to meet soon.

Flights were delayed and consolidated. Apparently it was snowing in New Jersey. When we finally left, there were no empty seats. The man beside me yammered endlessly, and illegally, into a cell phone. I was tempted to complain to the stewardess, a morbid brunette with a churned, Midwestern accent. I felt anxious. Ada's voice had materialized from too far in the past. My seat mate kept sniffling and swiping his nose, and by the time we touched down in Newark, I had a sore throat.

I phoned Shelley to tell her I'd arrived. Then a cab whirled me through the late February snow to the apartment on Grove Street, two blocks from the place where I'd grown up. We had moved around the time I started high school. Not one store on Broad Street looked familiar.

Viktor the Spinner—I'd been searching for the name we used to call him. His nostrils flared, vacuuming in the exhaled smoke so it swirled through the lungs a second time.

"She'll tell you," he said wearily.

Tassels of long gray hair splattered over his neck. His blue eyes looked like they had just been watered.

The walls were hung with Alex's drawings and paintings. I walked around the room for a closer look: an oil of an old man with a long moustache walking a horse by the river nested between portraits of Viktor in a fedora and Alex's older brother, Paul. The paintings were bright and included various surreal elements: Viktor's face, for instance, appeared emerging from an oven.

Their outlines contrasted with the drabness of the mismatched and oddly arranged furniture. Several ladder-backed cane chairs stood in a semi-circle, as though for a study group.

Ada returned wearing a long black sweater with white mother-of-pearl buttons over her black dress.

"Sit," she said to me. "Go to your room, Viktor."

Obedient as a butler, Viktor turned on his heels.

"Why did you call me?"

"Sit," she repeated, settling back into her plush maroon armchair.

That was when I noticed: her eyes had not blinked once. They may have reflected light but they did not let any in.

For all practical purposes, Ada was blind.

Putting my coat down on the chair beside me, I did as I was told.

"Viktor stepped out of the apartment to buy sugar for the cook, who was baking a cake," she began. "We didn't see him again for twenty years. That was just how things were in 1942. I was in the kitchen, watching the cook make dinner. I sat near the stove, which didn't give much heat, so it was even colder than this. From December to April everyone wore coats. The cook stirred her soup with a fox draped around her neck."

Grubby from travel, I wanted to wash. I hadn't heard a war story in years; I'd forgotten how they used to overwhelm me with their lack of resolution. Ada. My window on the past. Stained glass. Without her, it would have remained a series of close-ups, a museum filled exclusively with portraits of one's own family.

"After my brother left, I leaned against the stove and tried reading. Impossible. I closed my eyes and smelled the vegetables, the little bits of meat. I was sorry there was still enough to go around. I looked forward to the day the shortages would eliminate all of it. I'd been a vegetarian for months. Of course I was a pacifist. It was a male pastime, this war."

I tried imagining living in a state of perpetual emergency.

"At night Father came back from the *Rathaus* where he worked as a judge. The cake was for his birthday, but everyone forgot it. By that time, we knew something was wrong. Mother had returned from the doctor's earlier with her own news (which she kept to herself for a couple of days). Now she went out immediately to look for Viktor. She'd done the rounds of prisons during the last war searching for Father. As she'd found him, she'd reason to feel confident she would recover her son. She visited the police station across the street; she checked the hospitals, the secret police, friends in the underground. By the time she came home, Father'd gone out again to confer with his contacts. Mother and I were still awake when he entered the room, his face drawn. He'd learned that Viktor had been arrested, not for buying sugar on the black market but for trying to cross the border a few miles away. They'd taken him to the capital. There was nothing we could do. We had to get some sleep. Even during a war, people slept.

"Years later, my brother came back. By then, we were living in New Jersey. His time in Siberia didn't do him much good. Twenty years. And now," she looked straight at me, half-smiling again, "how many years later, here you are. Our prodigal. You haven't, I hope, been to Siberia."

Her ironies clearly pleased her because Ada beamed.

A dog barked in the apartment downstairs. I looked around, blinking. Late afternoon, windows strafed with flakes, darkening.

"Why did you call me?"

"I have another story."

"Ada," I insisted.

"It's a good one. About a prostitute. You'll like it."

"I've heard it." Years ago, at the Black Pond Resort.

"You have?"

"If you don't tell me, I'm leaving."

Her features darkened. I felt a flicker of her anger.

"How many years, and he can't spare a few minutes," she said to no one in particular.

"How long?"

"What?"

"Since you could see."

Her fingers twitched.

"It's my son."

"What about him?"

"There," she said, gesturing down the hall. "In my room."

"What?" I rose.

"Wait," she said, leaning forward, her voice rising, more plea than command. "Wait," she said. Then, again, "Wait. There are things you should know."

Around me I felt the gaze of the horses, the dogs, the men in the paintings. Doubtless somewhere the fox too peered out from behind a juniper or a yew. Everyone was watching me, except Ada. My throat felt terribly tender. In different ways I had loved all the Kruks—they were my little Russian novel, so impulsive and uncontainable, you never knew if they were going to kiss you or bite you; around them, I was always alert, ready for anything.

And I sat back in my chair, which was small and uncomfortable, and thought about why I had come.

2

I got to know the Kruks the summer I turned ten, while vacationing in the Catskills. Everyone was still poor then. That they could even take vacations again stunned the immigrants who remembered hunger and the war and the years quarantined in Quonset huts in Germany awaiting word from Washington about their futures. Before that, they had been side bets for a dozen feuding tribes. They'd been hit hard: one out of four of their countrymen was dead. Separated by war, reunited in the States, thousands of miles from home, together they hunted the scattered pieces of cross and country, bound to each other more tightly than they knew. After all, the word family, as I later learned, comes from the Latin for slave.

The Black Pond Resort was a crescent of bungalows cupping a mud-hole that must have been fed by deep springs, because even that withering summer the water level never dropped. A choir loft of peepers, the pond was also infested with snakes. The snakes, however, recognized boundaries, haunting only the far end of the waterhole. Rarely did one bob beyond the tanning rock along the edge of which someone had strung a clothesline from shore to shore as a marker for kids.

We arrived Saturday afternoon and immediately set about carrying suitcases and boxes of food into the screened-in porch of our duplex bungalow. Father, tall and angular, practically fleshless, took off his hat and laid it on the shiny black hood of the car, then set to the heavy lifting.

Mother, who still wore her hair in two ankle-length braids that lashed her back, planted herself in the kitchen where she unpacked the cartons, setting out the Rice Krispies, pickled beets, frozen *piroby*, and condensed milk for the key lime pie she made every summer. The empty shelves were papered in yellow, crisp sheets on the bed were turned down, and a bouquet of orange lilies burned in a vase on the table. I'd set my suitcase on the cot in my own private room and returned to the car for the bag of comics and *Mad* magazines when a door in the adjoining house slammed and a slight boy with longish hair, green shorts, and black Keds zipped by, nodding as he passed.

Alex Kruk and I had been confirmed together three years earlier, after a century of Saturdays studying a Baltimore Catechism translated and adapted for the Byzantine Rite. Mass was conducted in Old Slavonic, a language no one understood. It wasn't clear whether or not the priest himself knew what he was saying. This made it easier to doze during the service. Alex and I weren't friends yet. He was thin, almost fragile, with a sharp chin and bright green eyes. His last name means raven, but at the time I remember thinking he looked more like an ant. In religion class, he sat in the back while I colonized the front. I recall him mumbling the Little Doxology while the jowly deacon growled, "Spit the stones out now, boy," invoking me as an example, which seemed unfair since Alex attended public school while I was enrolled at St. Clements.

Halfway down the hill, he stopped and called out: "Dontcha wanna see the game?"

I looked to Father.

"Go ahead, Nicholas," he said.

Summer had officially begun. I pursued Alex down, then up a ridge at the top of which we found a soccer match in progress. Eight men and boys, four on each team, were scattered across a freshly mowed field swamped in sunlight. I recognized most of the faces from church—lean, sharp cheeks, large noses, and bad teeth—though the rigor of play elicited an intensity of expression rarely evoked by Sunday Mass.

They played rough. Friends tripped friends; brothers collided, ramming shoulders with the weight of real grievance. One pair in particular tangled more than the rest: a tall pimply boy wearing a white guinea-T mixed it up with the goalie, a stocky, muscled man in a blue sky cap. They were on the same team.

Alex stood beside a woman in a broad-brimmed straw hat that contrasted with the kerchiefed heads around her. I recognized his mother, Adriana Kruk, about whom I'd heard my parents whispering—stories that were cut short when I appeared. The sort one wanted to know. Her jaw was square as a terrier's. She had high Slavic cheeks. Her nose and lips were fleshy and her long eyes flashed green and gold. She looked like a thicker Marlene Dietrich.

A cry drew my attention back to the field. The goalie and the pimply boy were at each other again. This wasn't unusual: in our neighborhood, street soccer was basic training. The shoving had gone a step further—the goalie knocked the kid down, and the teenager stuck one leg between the man's feet then used his other as a hook to yank his opponent into the grass. They scuffled on the ground until the man managed to drive the boy's face into the stubble and, riding his back, twist his knobby elbow up into his shoulder. Their lips never stopped moving. Finally the older man rose and, with a last kick, turned away. No sooner had he shown his back than the boy was on him, wringing his neck.

"That's enough. Leave your father alone, Paul."

Mrs. Kruk had barely raised her voice, yet she'd been heard. Paul was Alex's older brother. The goalie was their father Lev, whom everyone called "the old revolutionary." I called him that too even though I had no idea what it meant. I'd heard my parents saying it. They'd say, "And did you hear what that old revolutionary said then?" And, "I wouldn't want to get that old revolutionary mad at me." This was the first time I'd seen the old revolutionary—who could not have been over forty—in action. He never came to church with his family.

Mrs. Kruk's command shattered the spell that had settled over the players. Lev cuffed Paul on the cheek and the game resumed.

We watched many matches that week. Most featured at least one brawl between father and son. Afterwards, if Lev's team won, Ada (as everyone called Adriana) and Alex beamed at the winners, though Alex seemed shyer in victory. If they lost, their dour expressions might not fade until the bonfire, a nightly ritual at which the vacationers gathered to sing and reminisce about the old world.

These evenings sometimes expanded into mini-vaudevilles and included recitations of poems, maudlin songs performed by an *a Cappella* quartet, and elaborate anecdotes about friends who hadn't survived the war. Ada got up and told the story about a client of her father's who was thrown in jail and used the time in prison to make boxes out of the bread his jailors brought him, beautiful things with intricate patterned inlays, which he had delivered to his creditors the day after he was shot.

She was a popular raconteur. One of her most memorable recitals was the story about the prostitute. As a fire licked poplar bark so it crackled like bacon behind her, Ada rushed on: "There's one night in Vienna, before we went to the displaced persons camp. I was waiting for someone to arrive at the train station, maybe Lev," she gestured at her husband.

"I started talking to this girl. Eighteen, maybe? She had red hair, a thick mouth. How old was I? Sixteen? I forget. My German wasn't good but I wanted to know. I saw right away what she was: her blouse was open, and her lips were violent as sunsets seemed in those days. One of her legs was in a cast. I asked her why she did what she did, and about her leg. Maybe because I was younger, she didn't get angry. It must have been a quiet night, or maybe she was already done, the meter off.

"She told me how boring everything was: the war, her life, the men she was with. Little tormented her; nothing surprised her. Nothing caught her unprepared, no man made her heart beat faster, no dawn left her wondering what turns life might take. Her life had no seasons, she said. Once a man kissed her hand and she slapped him. She thought he was making fun of her. To her surprise, he didn't hit her back. Instead, he spent the night. He had a pencil mustache, she said. Looked British, though of course he was German. Turned out, he was a paratrooper.

"The next morning he invited her to go up in the plane with him. 'We can fall through the sky together,' he'd offered. She'd never been in a plane, much less used a parachute, but she'd always wanted to touch a cloud. He swore there was nothing to it. They were drinking—during the war, most everyone was drunk most of the time—and he found some friends who were also drinking and who were able to get ahold of a plane somewhere.

"It was a clear bright cloudless day. There were a few other girls, a few other soldiers. The soldiers were all quickly telling girls what they should do, how they should land.

"Then he helped her on with the parachute and attached it to some line or something, I don't remember the details, and they jumped out of the airplane together, holding hands. He pulled their ripcords at the same time. Only, his didn't open. She remembered the moment hers burst against the blue sky with a whump, yanking her up so she had to let go of his hand.

"She said she heard him scream: 'What should I do? What should I do?' In German. She said if she had had a knife she would have cut the ropes of her chute. Instead, she watched the earth grow larger, and thought how beautiful it was, and when she landed, she broke her leg and lay in the field for a long time before she managed to crawl to a farm house."

The émigrés always talked about places none of us kids had ever seen, telling stories we couldn't quite imagine, in a language spoken, near as we could tell, nowhere else on earth outside our homes. Their stories sometimes didn't make sense, and weren't entirely coherent. What had happened to the soldier? Why hadn't the girl been killed? For us the old country was alternately Atlantis, Oz, or Devil's Island, looming so large in our parents' minds that it fell like an iron curtain between us. Our immediate world—a reality swarming with armed bees, bright orange salamanders, and pastel butterflies—had as little presence for most of them as their grief did for us. They seemed stricken by tunnel vision, and walked through the days with their minds fixed on some point in the past. Meanwhile around us flowered the fabulous flora of America at its peak. We squirmed and poked at each other—but there was no escaping the grownups, who forced us to recite verse in their language: *Tilke ya, mov okayaniy, i den i nich plachu.* I alone, the cursed one, weep day and night. Who was he? Why was he weeping? They told us, but we kept forgetting, distracted by the sparks flying up into a sky crowded with sputniks and stars. Only Alex and Paul didn't sit with the other kids. The Kruks moved as a pack, huddling around the fire like restive wolves.

After the bonfire, the children were sent to sleep, though who drifted off early in the mountains? When the door closed, I went to the window to watch bats surfing the treetops and fireflies in the field, like a million eyes blinking in the dark. I thought about the prayers I'd just said: Our Father, and Mary, and Jesus—all of whom were so nice, I never had to be afraid, thanks to them—they heard every word. They stood beside me at all times. They were in the room and they were outside with the fireflies. They would protect us from the Russians. They would help our aunts and our cousins trapped in the old country. I always said an extra set of Hail Marys for my grandmother, Father's mother, whom he hadn't seen in fifteen years. And then I stared into the dark, waiting for the world to open, for Grandmother to step out from the shadows.

My bed was in the corner, against the wall, on the other side of which lived the Kruks. Often I was wakened by shouts from their kitchen: Alex's screams, Paul's curses, Lev's growls. I knew he beat them. Most parents beat their children. The ones who didn't, like mine, were looked down on as soft.

When he wasn't playing soccer Lev stalked the grounds with a cigar in his mouth, the beak of his cap yanked down. The veins in his biceps were violet. I used to stare at the scarred tissue under his eye where, it was rumored, a bullet had grazed him.

Alex never mentioned the beatings, even when a bruise blued his cheek. It was hard to imagine how his bones did not crack under the blows: they looked so angular and thin. Instead, he chattered nervously, and led me to the well near the barn where he said a little girl had fallen in and drowned the previous summer. He said people thought she'd been pushed. Nobody knew by whom. He insisted you could hear her if you tried. We stuck our heads into the black shaft and listened.

"Hear?" he asked.

Only peepers.

"She's trying to tell us who pushed her. Listen."

Strain as I might, the rest was silence.

"You can't hear it?" Alex shook his head. "Hey, you know what?"

"What?"

"Sounds like she's saying your name." He smirked, and ran off.

The crack upset me. How could the girl have guessed I was called Nicholas? Had we met in school or church? At night I asked Mother what she knew about the business and she assured me Alex had been teasing.

That first summer, the Kruk brothers also taught us to play Secret Police. It was a game in which you drew lots to determine who would be a civilian and who a spy. You alone knew which you were. One person was designated the Body. The Body hid somewhere, preferably deep in the woods, after telling just one other player where he'd be. That player, in whom the Body confided, might be a civilian or a spy. The player who knew then tried to lead his team to the Body. What he didn't know, however, was just who was on his team and who was the enemy. The game was a graduate education in paranoia. During my turns hiding, I quickly felt abandoned, forgotten by the others. I hated myself for feeling this way and mumbled one of the solemn, violent poems I'd learned in Saturday school.

"... meet to bless thee, Mother of God, ever-blessed and most immaculate Mother of God. Higher in honor than the Cherubim and incomparably more ..."

Mosquitoes ruined any chance of concentration. I swatted my knee and tweaked my ear and Alex and I began slipping back from the hundreds of people huddled in an amphitheater of rocks before the outdoor chapel whose onion dome glowed. Towering pines surrounded the worshippers arrayed on a floor of glistening copper needles while shafts of light flecked the scene. What if a sudden beam were to strike the chalice? A crack of lightning would follow, heaven would open, and who knows? In this air anything was possible.

" ... accept our prayers and present them to Thy Son and our God, that for thy sake He may save and enlighten our sons ..."

Several hundred stood rapt in the booming voice of the bald priest while we detached ourselves. I took one last glance at Mother—crosshatched in light, Father beside her, his face a mirror of concentration, as though this meant something to them—and we were off deep into the woods to find the Man in the Tower. The bright air trembled with flies that might have been miniature angels as we scrambled over mossy rocks and hillocks, plunging farther into the fabulous. Will the world ever again seem so riven with possibility and penetrated by dream as it did that morning?

When the echoes of the Mass were supplanted by the cheerier musings of whippoorwills and blackbirds, we slowed.

"That's the mark," Alex said, pointing to a dab of blue paint on the trunk of a pine.

"And there," I said, spying another up ahead.

We navigated by trees as easily as if we were strolling the orderly streets of New York. Only our destination remained unclear: we knew that somewhere not too far stood a water tower converted into a dwelling in which lived a famous old poet. He'd survived two wars and the Famine, and now he sat in his tower room, writing, supported by a community of friends who believed him about important business. I'd seen him once at a concert in Carnegie Hall. Mother had pointed him out, and the reverence in her voice impressed me. Rumor was that he wrote and prayed all day and all night and that he never needed to switch on the lamp because of the light emanating from his own head. It was said that Sundays after Mass he welcomed visitors. We had no intention of talking to him and hoped only to lure him from his lair for a closer look.

After walking past a mosquito-infested bog and up a small hill, we came to a clearing. The old tower resembled a giant wine cask set on a tripod. No doubt it had once supplied water for the community. Next year I would enter the sixth grade and come face to face at last with the dreaded Sister Capone, as the kids called her: good now to practice courage.

We approached slowly. Fear shook me—the same fear I've always felt when stepping out of bounds. Just what boundary was I about to transgress? Alex scooped stones.

"Get some," he said.

We planned to pelt the tower until the poet emerged. Seeing him would complete our mission.

"God's day to you, boys."

The voice behind us cut through to our hearts.

We turned.

"Nice to have visitors," he smiled.

He wore denim overalls, like the beekeeper in that children's book, *The Custodian of Clandestine Flowers*. White hair sprouted everywhere, even from his ears. He coddled a pipe in his hands.

We stood ready for flight. Up close, the poet appeared tiny. Two of us could take him. I nudged Alex, who suddenly had nothing to say.

The old man shuffled nearer, until I could smell the tobacco on his breath. His teeth were yellow as a sunflower.

"You know what the Greek used to say: Stay silent or say something better than silence."

He scratched his nose.

"Want to see the tower?"

"Yes sir," Alex finally said.

"Good."

He led us up the ladder. About fifteen feet off the ground there was a landing, but before we reached it I smelled something terrible and heard a buzzing of flies. Approaching the doorway, I feared we were entering a hive.

The place was dark but the stench was so sharp that my throat tightened and the buzzing made it impossible to hear what the old man was saying. An alley of light from the door lit stacks of books and papers.

"Yes, let there be light, yes," the old man shouted, pushing open a window.

There were flies everywhere and when the window opened most of them streamed out.

What had drawn them wasn't immediately clear because the onslaught made me leap to the side and topple a tower of books and papers and ink pots with quill pens, and it seemed like every inch of floor and desk was covered with books and papers and quills, many of which had stoles or muffs resting on them like paperweights—until I saw that the furs were attached to noses, and heads, and feet, and tails, and what I took to be quills were in fact small arrows. All around us were heaped the corpses of dead and decomposing squirrels and raccoons and rabbits and birds and other small game. The floor was black with dried blood and ants.

The old man seemed oblivious to the horror and began pushing us deeper in, but I'd made my decision. I bolted out and down the ladder and raced for the woods, and it wasn't until I saw the outdoor chapel, now deserted, which we'd left half an hour ago, that I turned to find Alex behind me.

Breathless, I stopped and sank onto a stone, heart pounding.

We looked at each other. What was there to say? We'd been warned not to go and now we knew why.

Blessed Mary Mother of God, keep us always from harm.

⁓

The first signs of Alex's vocation were the comics he drew on long strips of yellow paper, which he then cut into panels, taping the cells together into a sequence and turning them into a homespun film. He cut slits in both ends of a shoe box and threaded his strip through them, allowing us to watch our own version of television. Some of the strips were about his father: Father as ogre with one eye; Father with horns; Father wielding a knife. Alex previewed these at private screenings, myself the audience. At the end, I always applauded.

⁓

"I love my father," Alex said when I asked him the riddle.

"But who would you rather die first anyway, your father or your mother?" It was a game I'd learned at school. Impossible to answer but a pleasure to pose. We were sitting by the pond, stick-poles in water.

"They don't die," he finally said.

Too squeamish to spear a worm, I'd tied mine in a noose. "What do you mean?"

"They go to heaven."

"Not everybody."

"My father says there's no such place as hell. Or purgatory."

"Then which would it be?"

But his loyalty was clear. I would get no answer from him.

One of the other boys ran up and said, "Come on, they're starting the game!"

3

As it turned out, that summer was the last time I saw "the old revolutionary." By the following year, Adriana Kruk had become something unheard of in émigré circles: a divorcee. Her husband, Lev, had moved in with a nineteen-year-old girl, a receptionist at the plant.

In Roosevelt, walking home Sundays after Mass, my parents discussed Khrushchev and Kennedy. They also talked a lot about Ada, who seemed determined to shock her fellow parishioners into the present with strange hats and slit skirts. It was the sixties, though she was the only one in our circle to register the change.

"Remember what happened to her father," my father said, defending Mrs. Kruk.

"What?" I asked.

"It's not for children," Mother said.

"He should know," Father countered.

"Later. When he's older," Mother said, closing the matter.

The following August, on the ride up to the Catskills, Mother repeated how we had to be nice to the Kruks. Lev's leaving had been a terrible thing. She'd heard the boys were going wild. Ada didn't know how to control them.

"Isn't there anybody else you can play with?" she asked. "They're not a good match for you." This was the start of a refrain that crescendoed over the next months.

My forehead heated the glass. People slogging down sidewalks changed to cows in meadows. Every so often I studied Father gripping the wheel. Thick black brows met above his nose like linked fingers. If he were to run away or die, who would drive the car? Who would take me to the hospital, or haul the groceries up the stairs? Could Mother manage us alone? Somehow I doubted it. I felt sad for Alex, and scared for myself, and I resolved to be his friend. Alex at ten was still tiny and loose-limbed, and you didn't need a crystal ball to know that, unlike his athletic brother Paul, he was headed for trouble. I mean, he had nerve, no doubt of that. He had a yen, he wanted action. And he was pleasant to look at, with chestnut bangs and an eager stare. When he concentrated, his face puckered, his ample lips kissed the air, and his eyes narrowed around his crooked yet noble nose. He was fast but clumsy, as though he were at war with himself, and you couldn't help wondering what voices barked what orders in his head.

At a rest stop on the Turnpike, I strayed into a patch of pines whose bark peeled like burnt skin. The trees had seen everything, met all kinds. Beyond them, in a clearing, loomed the shell of a house partly gutted by fire. A paneless window frame hung in the air. Peering in, I spied a piano with a mouthful of broken keys; a naugahyde recliner, the stuffing ripped out; the iron frame of a bed in which a couple once frisked. Returning to the car, I found what I hoped was a finger bone, but when I showed it to Father, whose authority on all matters from stocks to roses startled everyone, he assured me it was merely the spine of a squirrel.

As we neared the Black Pond that second summer, my sorrow veered to euphoria. I remembered our games, Secret Police, and the pond. By the time we pulled up to our old bungalow, I was smiling.

Afternoons, Adriana Kruk sat by the pond crowned in that huge straw hat under which coiled masses of lush, violently dyed blond hair. She may have been at the peak of her beauty—it happens to divorcees, a kind of second blooming. Her skin took gold from the sun as her due. Whatever hardships she suffered after Lev left she kept to herself. Abandonment suited her.

Semen, who'd worked in the factory with Lev, noticed me staring at his old flame.

"You should have seen her twenty years ago. Prettiest girl in the camps. Everyone gathered around her. We were like the snakes in the pond. Such eyes, such charm."

Ada, sitting across the pond, turned to Semen and said:

"Are you going to town this afternoon?"

"Just give me a list. Whatever you need," Semen said.

"Thank you. Isn't it nice in the sun? Could be anywhere." She adjusted her sunglasses and dropped the straps of her suit.

Ada worked as a waitress back in Roosevelt.

"You know," Semen added, his voice pitched high remembering a lost passion, then dropping, "she doesn't understand what's happened to her. She's still trying to live the old life. She's hoping things will take care of themselves." He said, more to himself than to me. "You have to want to enter America."

"And," added Mrs. Gvalt, who'd been listening to our conversation. "You have to remember where you come from."

"Semen, more lotion."

"Certainly."

I watched as Semen walked over and, dripping the *Ban de Soleil* on his palms, rubbed Ada's fleshy brown shoulders. After a few minutes, she said:

"Thank you," stopping his hand with her long fingers. "I should just go see what the boys need."

She sat up abruptly and retied her suit.

I watched her walk slowly to her cabin, back glistening, her fine legs measuring every step.

A few minutes later, Semen got up.

"Should get ready. You want anything from the store? You want to come too?" He asked me.

"No thanks."

The snake's side of the pond was thick with reeds and lilies blooming from a muddy bottom—of the sort that, if you touched it, your foot slipped immediately into a lubricated suction cup of slime. The Jello-ey slipperiness of algae was soothing and creepy, as though you were plumbing a mouth. One afternoon, under a hot sun, we were splashing in the shallows guarded by a sleepy heron crowning the oak when we noticed the periscope of a baby snake in our waters. Alex gave chase. The snake moved slowly, as though teasing him on. I watched Alex's body melt into the water, from ankle to knee to the small of the back to shoulders, until he was swimming past the line, his prey a black muscle, hooking along the rippling surface. Too slowly, the adults caught on to the game. By then, he was snakeside, the green water darkening, his limbs flying. We mocked him. "What a goober," someone said.

He caught it. Treading water, he hoisted his trophy high. For a second, the world was still. We stared at the writhing black bolt. Then, from overgrown banks, from bobbing lily pads and flexing reeds, a half-dozen brown snakes darted forth and lunged at him. The one in his hand curled and jabbed his wrist. Alex screamed.

My father was the first to reach him. Mrs. Kruk had frozen. She stood with fingers screening her mouth, her other arm at her side, the hand opening and shutting like a heart. Her eyes more angry than scared. I didn't know yet how intimate she was with emergency.

Then Alex was in our car, one arm camouflaged in a red towel, the other a blue one, and we were racing up to Kingston in the Chrysler's cloth-cushioned cave. Adriana sat silent and pale in back, holding her son, who sobbed softly, more from confusion than pain. On his other side sat my mother. I was up front, head out the window, grimacing at the corn. I felt guilty. I'd done nothing to stop Alex. I'd watched him the way I'd watched Paul and Lev fight over soccer. I looked at the red coin on my finger. Before Mother had bandaged him, I'd reached over and touched Alex, wanting to feel the blood. I'd quickly brought my finger to my nose, sniffed it, then brushed my hand on my trunks. But not all of it had been wiped away. I began to pray. Religious beggar. *God, help my friend*. I promised Him that if He did, I'd be kinder to everyone, even our neighbor's cat. Barns ticked by.

In Kingston an intern from India with an exotic British accent corroborated my father's claim: the snakes weren't poisonous. "I've never heard of such a thing," he said. "In my country, snakes are solitary creatures. Do you think they belonged to a union?" He clucked at his witticism.

Despite the dozen or so bites over his arms and chest, and the locks of blood, Alex was more frightened than hurt. After bandaging and one tetanus shot, he was released. We must have been a sight in that rural ward—six people in bathing suits and flip flops. Only Father had bothered to grab a jacket, which now hung loose over his lean, shirtless frame.

On the ride back, Adriana recovered herself. With her son out of danger, she gradually reclaimed the stage. This time it was Alex who sat, stiff and sober, sandwiched between two cold-skinned women in bathing suits. Adriana was covered with goose bumps and I tried not to follow their trail along her arm to the breasts straining the taut synthetic of her red suit.

"Turn around and roll up your window, Nicholas," my mother insisted.

"I remember the day the Germans arrived," Mrs. K said, as though in response to a question. "We were picnicking by the River Pamiat outside town. Suddenly there was Viktor. He was just a boy. He wore a suit; his shirt was soaked. He told us the war had finally arrived. Remember where you were, Slava?" she asked my mother.

Mother ignored her.

"Slava. Only a few summers after we met. Remember?"

"No," mother replied, slamming the door yet again, as she often did, without any explanation, on the past.

The past was a minefield about which few maps seemed to agree. And why should that surprise me? It's a big place.

⁓

The milk truck had come and gone when I went next door to get Alex. My parents were taking us to the general store in Kerhonkson, miles from Black Pond.

Adriana opened the screen. Her blond hair rose in a corona, while bunched above her waist her blue dress swelled with promises. She looked down at me and said warmly: "I have a photograph of Jesus. Would you like to see it, Nicholas?"

"Sure," I said, wondering why my mother had never shown me such a thing.

I walked through the porch to the kitchen. The place smelled of rusty tins. Corn husks poked withered green ears from the trash. On the table sat a stack of photo albums.

"I don't think so," said Alex, appearing at her side.

"I want to see it," I said, afraid he'd misunderstood.

"Look. Look at this," Adriana said, producing a postcard-sized black and white picture of Jesus among the lambs and passing it to me.

I held the precious evidence in my hands.

"I have more," she said softly. "These are all pictures of God." She gestured to the albums on the table. I stared at her, strangely stirred.

"It's a drawing," Alex said curtly.

"Give your mother a kiss," Adriana whispered, taking back her card.

Before I knew what I was doing, I leaned forward and stamped my lips on her cheek.

Her head jerked back and her eyes blinked twice.

My friend frowned. "I'm not going," he said.

"Why not?"

"Because," Alex replied, retreating.

His battle was not with his father.

Alex's brother, Paul, scared me now. Four years older, a teenager, his irises seemed to saturate the whites of his eyes with their blackness. This year there were no soccer games. Instead, every so often, Paul threw fits. One morning I was awakened by a crack at my window. I got up and looked outside. The sun was just rising over the mountain in the distance and mist from the pond fringed the bungalows. Near the well stood Paul, wearing shorts and a T-shirt. He was picking up pebbles from the driveway and flinging them at the cottage panes, as though daring one of the adults to come out and confront him. Finally, my father did. As he approached, Paul cocked his arm, but when my father spoke, Paul slowly relaxed. He dropped the stones, turned, and ran into the woods that waited at the edge of the clearing like the arms of wildness itself.

That morning at breakfast Father and Mother discussed again how Lev's sudden departure was affecting the boys.

This time, the Kruks were accompanied by Adriana's brother, Viktor, whom we called the Spinner. We called him that because every so often Viktor stopped in his tracks, threw out his arms, and spun around, like a roulette wheel whirled by an invisible hand. He was then a skinny man in his late thirties with a horsy face that reminded me of Stan Laurel. He'd emerge from the bungalow late in the day, bottle in hand, wearing a tired gray wool suit, a soiled white shirt, no tie, and an embittered fedora. He would set himself up in a green Adirondack chair near the pond, a stack of newspapers and an ashtray beside him, and for the rest of the day he would sit, smoking, replenishing his glass of wine often enough that by supper two and sometimes three bottles nestled in the high grass at his feet. Every so often he would get up, stretch out his arms, and spin. After saying good morning, the other vacationers ignored him. The only adult I ever saw engage with him was my mother. But Mother talked with everybody, and not just people—we'd spied her discoursing with birds, squirrels, trees. I was relieved that when Viktor rose for a spin, she stayed put. She was a large woman and the sight of her making like a whirligig might have killed me.

Viktor didn't say much, but when he did open his mouth, almost invariably it was to deliver a short speech on Stalin and Truman, about whom he joked as though they had all been classmates at a prep school in hell.

"You know about the mother of I. Vissarianovich Dzhugashvili, don't you, my boy? Stalin, son, Stalin. Of Gori, Georgia. They say his mother's morals weren't all they might have been—especially given that Georgia was home to one of the world's earliest Christian communities. Three wise men appear candidates for the part of the tyrant's father: a prince, a general, and a prosperous local businessman whom the old lady served as a part-time maid. The legal *pater*, however, taught the boy much in the way of contempt for the species.

"It was a curious household: the father beat mother and son, the mother beat the father and son, and the son waited a few years before taking it out on thirty million in the name of Mother Russia, who was no more his mother than his father had been his father, and whose language he didn't even know until he was nine."

Without pausing, he went on to balance his equation:

"Harry Truman, on the other hand, was said to be a mama's boy. His mother was his first chief of staff: 'Now Harry, you be good,' she counseled him. His father also had a temper. When Harry fell off a pony, his father made him walk the rest of the way. His teachers had names like Mira Ewin and Minnie Ward. I'm not sure how much names tell us, but if the devil had a name, could it ever be Minnie? History was Truman's passion. He read all two thousand books in the town library. His heroes were primarily generals, from Hannibal to Robert E. Lee. Biographers agree that Truman was *fond* of people. None of this made any difference when the time came to drop the bomb.

"And, for the longest time, he and Stalin liked each other!"

Lunch was a communal affair held around wormy picnic tables under the pines. A conspiracy of mothers covered the table with plastic-coated cloth and paper plates. At noon, a battery of dishes materialized: there was cold borscht, of course, alongside sausages and ham and homemade bread. Sliced tomatoes were covered with bland white onions shriveled from the heat. Flies peppered the potato salad, and once I found a banana slug mapping an ear of corn. Mother's key lime pie was everyone's favorite.

Despite the mosquitoes thriving in the shade, people lingered, gossiping and arguing about the war, the old country, communists.

The senseless conversation of grownups.

Mother was telling the table what her doctor said about the child she'd lost that spring. She rarely mentioned yesterday and had never before spoken of her miscarriage in front of me, though I'd a vague sense of it. Several months back, I came home from school to find Semen at the apartment. "Your mother's had to go to the hospital," he said, without elaborating. When she returned home she was very quiet and didn't want to talk about it beyond telling me not to expect any brothers or sisters too soon.

"No brother for Nicholas. The doctor said."

"Well, he's a Jew, so he should know," Semen said.

Mother's eyes flashed angrily.

"I had a letter from Anton," Ada offered.

Everyone turned to her. Anton was the poet who later inspired Ada to wallpaper her apartment with English hunting scenes. After the war he'd gone to London instead of New York.

"And?" Semen asked.

"He hopes to visit New York around Christmas."

"We'll organize an evening for him," the crowd murmured in rare harmony.

We waited for the grownups to finish so we could hurry off to our games.

One day, after supper, a troop of us were playing Secret Police, scouting for the Body. The night before, several kids claimed to have seen a devil chasing girls in white gowns across the field. We were anxious. Twilight, when things lose their boundaries and start melting into each other, drifted down slowly, like someone lazily smearing a blackboard. The moment was turning. Edward, our leader, had given the signal to retreat when suddenly Andrew, who was ahead, waved for us to join him. We hurried over to the edge of the clearing. There we saw Viktor the Spinner with one of the older boys, sitting on a toppled, half-rotten oak, talking. Viktor, in his uniform suit and fedora, raised a bottle to his lips. The boy, who was smoking a cigarette, shaped stories with his fingers and rocked back and forth, but we were too far to hear anything. Then, as though someone had popped the lid on a jack-in-the box, Viktor rose up and extended his arms. I noticed he had a cigarette in each hand. He shut his eyes, and his feet began rotating. Soon he was spinning. The boy laughed. Instinctively we looked at Alex, who refused to acknowledge us and was the first to turn away. As there seemed nothing more to see, we followed. Across the dirt road along the field, behind a sagging fence, a black bull with stocky horns studied us.

There seemed nothing more to see, but there was clearly more to know. The last night of our second upstate summer fell on my eleventh birthday. The afternoon was full of Go Fish, Freeze Tag, and Cake. When it grew dark, we gathered in front of the barn for a farewell fire. We'd dragged in logs and twigs from the woods, then built a pyre twice my size. Stewed in gasoline, the pyramid ignited with a loud woosh, exploding like a billion bulbs. Across from me stood the Kruks: golden-haired Adriana, Viktor in his fedora, Paul and Alex gawky in shorts. In the startled light we all looked at each other as though into a mirror. Shadows shot up behind them, and it seemed as though the past, time itself, had suddenly found a body.

The Disappearing Sickness

1

Back in Roosevelt, we ran into the Kruks at St. Clements. Every Sunday the flaking gold onion-domes spilled old and recent émigrés into the streets. Who would have thought them bright days for the community? Overwhelmed by the new world, people replied to external forces by fanning a missionary, inward flame. They gathered in God's name and their common purpose charged each soul with practical zeal. Only Mother fought the pull of the past. "We're in New Jersey, for God's sake," she repeated. "America. America."

Father beamed. His mantra was "It's never too late to start saving," and he once explained to me that the only way to work through your own suffering was by relieving someone else's. He celebrated everything Mother did, from the borschts she boiled to the clothes she chose for him, including even her fits at his overindulgence of her.

Whatever may have happened to her in the old country, Mother insisted on enjoying things. It is a rare capacity. While

Father worked and dozed through medical school classes, Mother reveled in feeding both her family and the birds, crushing crusts on porch railings; she loved shopping and never griped about the chores that owned her, from five in the morning until long after I had gone to bed. She overpaid, undercooked, and swapped gossip with the salesgirl at the A & P. These were her pleasures. She was big yet her size never slowed her: she ranged with the grace of a dancer while looking more like a diva.

She was at home in that neighborhood of neat gray and green triple deckers, with clotheslines wiring balconies like ropes in a circus or the masts of a ship forever tossing on turbulent waters—more so than she ever felt in Fort Hills. Clumps of grass sprouted from sidewalks salted with glass; trellises and arbors of steel pipes propped roses, tomatoes, blooming vines. In Roosevelt, the buildings leaned into each other for comfort, and found it. Communion in misery offered a solace the elaborate privacies of the burbs rarely matched.

The streets brimmed with personages, from Fran Parks, who planted pot in her window box, to Pietro, who'd been a painter in the Village before going to booze and personal demons and who now spent his days pacing Fulton Street costumed. Beginning Monday as Adam, he moved successively to Egyptian slave, Richard the Lionhearted, and Benjamin Franklin. Saturdays were unpredictable: maybe Hepburn, or why not Truman? Sundays he hit the street hauling a cross of tomato stakes over his shoulder. His madness was hardly charming. Occasionally he'd stand on the corner, shouting at passersby: "Ah, why dontcha go back where ya came from, ya friggin' Hunkies?" But there was no law against pretending each day was Halloween. So long as cousin Luke in Bayonne made the rent, Pietro dressed as he pleased. Besides, most families had one if not more Pietros to cope with.

My mother barreled her bulk down the halls and aisles of that world waving and tasting, taming and loving, often apologizing, and taking no bows.

2

Mother's attitude toward the Kruks continued to harden. She must have heard reports from neighbors. While she often murmured sympathetic sententia about her friend's circumstances, she urged me to spend more time with schoolwork and less with Alex. Only an outright prohibition, however, could have kept me from that house, whose attractions intensified along with the aura of anarchy enveloping it. At the Kruks' I learned to smoke, had my first taste of vodka, and decoded that siren song whose signals I felt but whose source had remained encrypted.

Alex, who'd inherited Ada's reckless imagination, told me he'd been born with a disease called the disappearing sickness. Ada also spoke of it, and I've subsequently heard one or two old country practitioners mention this colorful nonsense. The first months of his life, every morning, on waking, his skin would begin turning transparent until it seemed to have evaporated, leaving only a pulsing heap of vessels, muscles, and burgundy organs. It was as if some part of him wanted to stay asleep. The only way he could stop himself from disappearing entirely was by screaming.

Adriana was terrified. She took him to Dr. Hlib, who conducted the exam smoking a Pall Mall. His ashy fingers probed the boy's ears and anus, and when he was finished, he said, "Yes yes, *malus invisiblus*, the disappearing sickness. Don't see it much in America, though common as dust in the old country." He prescribed an expectorant, and told Adriana to wear earplugs if the screaming bothered her. She would have to endure it. It was simply the organism adapting to the world.

"The disease cures itself," the doctor explained.

Apparently he was right: one day, the screams turned into words. Alex insisted he uttered his first sentence before other kids could tell a thumb from a binkie.

"Ask Ada," he added.

By twelve, Alex had done with growing and was forced to learn his capacities. Neither Paul nor Lev had ever cut him any slack. He was expected to stand up to them; when he did, more often than not, he was slapped down. In response, he retreated into himself, into his drawings and fantasies, which imprinted themselves on his face, whose thick-lipped frailty was a singular hybrid of various Slavic slogans: high cheeks, a sharp Gogolian chin, limp dark hair, and large unlikely green eyes iridescent as wet leaves in sunlight. After a few minutes with him I'd be sucked into the cyclone of his obsessions, which, on his father's departure, grew legion. He became a compulsive collector, who pressed flowers, hoarded chestnuts like a squirrel, and clipped stamps off junk mail. He gathered matchbooks, beer bottles, pennies and stray bones: a row of tiny skulls from birds, squirrels, and raccoons edged his desk. Countless discarded and used-up objects found a home with Alex until the room he shared with Paul looked like a well-ordered dumpster behind a natural history museum. When he discovered girls, he swept the place clean and papered his wall with pin-ups. Years later, when he lost interest in things, it was partly a response to the surfeit of his adolescent trolling.

His quirks would have placated the most demanding neurotic. He was a compulsive hand washer who often wore gloves all day. He had at least a dozen pair, including three different colors in rubber, which he used while drawing, though most of the time he favored a cheap wool-lined brown suede.

And something about hair made him uneasy and led him to mock men whose nostrils were unkempt and to protest beards, and for a long time he refused to read Whitman because of the poet's inescapable hirsuteness. He kept his own eyebrows trimmed, and even as an adult he shaved three times a day—though by then he'd passed through a long-haired phase, which must have partly broken the spell.

His energy level never sagged. You imagined a child like that inspiring the inventor of Ritalin to work overtime. In his company I often felt myself fading away, stricken by my own form of the disappearing sickness. He was always on his way somewhere, always charging after some frog or skull or Indian head penny, whooping with excitement about the fifty cent match box car he found, or the pack of cigarettes someone had left behind on a bus. It didn't seem to matter what it was. Soon enough this rabid energy asserted itself in a curiosity about sex, which also hastened my own education.

On top of it, there was the indignity of history. Our parents were from a country that had all but disappeared after the war, and this had some singular consequences from which I was largely saved by attending the Catholic school associated with our church, where my troubles were confined to the more familiar complexes surrounding aggressive nuns and ardent deacons.

For Alex, on the other hand, school began the epic miseries of public life where the chemistry of beige tiles, ventilated lockers, hormone-addled kids, and rooms leached of warmth and personality was expected to generate an atmosphere that might nurture young souls.

"What's your name?" his fourth grade teacher asked sternly. Mrs. Linnaean was a long-faced woman with close cropped red hair, tufts of which sprouted like crabgrass from her ears, and whose corns and bunions made the days she spent on her feet a misery.

"Alex Kruk."

Small and thin, he still had the pallor of the sickly child despite his obvious vigor, and it seemed to annoy some of his teachers.

"Crook."

"K-r-u-k. U like in blue." Easy enough: What was the problem? His face reddened. He felt the others stare during the ritual humiliation that repeated itself annually: surely by now the whole school knew who he was and where he was from. But it didn't seem to work that way and every year he was forced to reinvent himself afresh for new teachers.

"What kind of a name is that?"

When he told her, she looked puzzled.

"Show the class on the map, Alex."

He went up to the front of the room. Classmates giggled at his short pants and drooping socks. His shoes were tight and his shirttail hung outside his clam-digger khakis. Shifting from foot to foot, he stared at the map, which seemed nothing like the one he'd studied at home. It wasn't there. Try as he might, he couldn't find the old country anywhere. Anxiety overwhelmed him: what would he say? What would he tell the teacher? She'd call him a liar, and would she be wrong? He wanted to erase himself the way Mrs. Linnaean swiped clean the board, and he tried willing the disappearing sickness to return.

"Not there," she said confidently. "That's Russia now."

When he reported what the teacher said, Adriana mocked him for letting himself be pushed around by people who needed to learn a little history.

"You weren't born a minority. You were born a boy." She told him again about the house by the sea and his grandfather the judge. She said their ghosts would come at night and stand on his head if he forgot them.

"Our people came to light in the twelfth century," she said, "Remember yourself."

Yet she felt overwhelmed. Her own son didn't believe what she told him about her past. Why would anyone else? And there was so much she never learned about her own parents, so much she never knew because they died relatively young, and she found herself filling in the blanks with stories improvised to answer the moment.

One gang seemed particularly offended by Alex, making the boys' rooms and deserted streets off school grounds treacherous zones. Once Mike Bryers and his buddies surrounded him, chanting, "He's a crook! Get the Kruk!" Paul happened by and, seeing his brother in trouble, hurried over. The hoods dispersed.

Paul pushed Alex with an open hand, saying, "Come on, kid. You gotta do better than that. Stand up for yourself. If you don't stand up for yourself, you'll go down. Don't you get it?"

The barrier separating the Kruks from their peers seemed breachable only through sports, and while Paul eventually broke through, Alex stayed on the outside, coddling anger and contempt for the teachers.

"Look," Paul said. "Some are born blind. Some are orphans. Some don't know what century they're in. Just deal."

"Next thing you'll start wanting to play baseball," Viktor moaned, wagging his head.

"They'll hate him if he doesn't," he added, sipping wine from a juice glass. "He should know that, Adriana, and you should too. There are things you do to fit in. And it's not only kids. Adults are worse."

Viktor nodded to himself, lighting a cigarette and sinking into the smoke. Thank God that was behind him. School in the old country was no better. There he'd learned subjects like the history of the Communist Party taught by soused party hacks. Spit on the bastards.

Then he said:

"Stalin studied to be a priest, you know. At a seminary in Georgia. The Russian rector over-monitored the boys. He broke into their lockers and had the boys put in detentions cells if he found any of the proscribed works. A paranoid atmosphere prevailed. Among the books that influenced him were the novels of Viktor

Hugo and Darwin's *The Descent of Man*. At twenty he failed to report for exams and was expelled. After that he devoted himself full time to revolutionary activities."

Turning to Truman, he noted:

"He was mild about religion. No fussing. He adored Mark Twain, the American humorist, and regarded politics as a dirty business but more interesting than chasing wealth. What good did it do a man to corner all the loose change in the world? You see what I'm getting at, son?"

Such was the counsel Alex received.

Year after year, class after class, Alex was forced to identify himself. Later, when he heard people complain about hyphenated Americans, he smiled—who put the hyphen there in the first place? Who was always making you self-conscious?

Like most young people, Alex felt persecuted merely for being himself: inside the cruel hallways of adolescence, everyone walks alone.

And from the start he felt encouraged only toward failure.

Finally, however, inspired by Viktor's and Paul's advice, and sick of feeling slighted, Alex discovered for himself what was in fact a familiar American tactic for annulling the past. That September, when his new homeroom teacher called his name, Alex raised a gloved hand and said:

"That's Kruko. Kruk-O!"

"Beg pardon?"

New to the school, she hoped to ingratiate herself with the students.

"K-R-U-K-O. It's Italian," he shrugged nonchalantly at the indifferent titters.

The woman looked at the registration list, shook her head, picked up a pencil, and recorded the correction.

And so, for the rest of his high school career, he became Alex Kruko, the Italian-American anti-athlete.

"Anti-athlete?" I asked.

"Like antipasto," he explained. "I'm against athletics. Look what it's done to my brother," he ground a finger against his forehead.

"See, you gotta take control. Can't just sit back. This is America, gumba."

His spontaneous decision to convert to Italian had surprising side effects. He seemed gradually taken in by his own pose. He began asking Ada to serve him only pasta; as she worked in an Italian restaurant, she found it easy to comply. And he took effervescent pride in the conquests of Julius Caesar and the voyages of Christopher Columbus, as though they really were, as he called them, paesanos.

"Hey, paesano," he'd shout to me out the window.

For a while it looked as though assimilation would run its natural course, and then some.

I was sitting at the breakfast table, surveying the platters of toast and cheese and tubs of butter and boxes of cereal Mother had set before me. When it came to food, Mother believed in abundance: our pantry was always bursting with six of everything: Rice Chex, packages of Ronzoni, and a wine cellar of ginger ale. She could have opened a distributorship with what we had on hand.

Mother was squeezing oranges when Rags, our cat, knocked at the window. Inside, he powdered our knees with the puff of his tail before settling down to a meal of fish heads, left over from the night before.

There was a knock on the door.

"It's Alex," Mother called, a frown in her voice.

Fleeing the army of breakfast foods, I raced to the door.

"Gotta go," I said.

"Where you going?"

"Frog for Pietro."

"What?"

"His experiments."

We raced down the stairs into the early summer light. Pietro, wearing a lab coat, had indeed asked us, gruffly, to find him a frog. I don't know who he was impersonating.

I'd run several blocks, dodging cars, waving to Mr. Pilsudski in the large smeared picture window of the tavern, which opened promptly at eight to give the men a pick-me-up before work, and he'd replied by saluting with his cigar, before I noticed Alex was dragging his feet. I slowed and waited for him to catch up.

"What's wrong?"

He glanced over both shoulders theatrically, then pulled out a pack of Camels. Pissed by his stalling, I snatched it from his hands and took off.

We ran down Broad Street.

Marco Polo might have spared himself some trouble and his king serious bucks had he known about Roosevelt, whose treasures stacked up against any in China: here was the Army/Navy store offering camping gear, mess kits, pocket knives. In the cabinet alongside the familiar Swiss numbers were gravity blades, and I remembered the time Billy the T got mad at me after religion class. He'd tracked me down, drawn a switchblade from his pocket, flicked it open, and pressed it to my neck. I don't remember being afraid. I knew he wouldn't hurt me, that what he wanted was a sign of submission, so I peed in my pants, and after that, for a few years everybody called me Leakey.

We galloped past a movie theater, to which I'd never gone, and the Kolber Sladkus shoe store whose owner, Mr. Green, was always friendly even though Mother would sometimes spend an hour trying on shoes before buying one pair of irregular socks at a discount. We passed the locksmith's, Jed's Liquors, Gimbels, three pizza parlors, a ridiculous number of hair salons, a wig emporium, and a five and dime. Sweating, I looked over my shoulder: Alex, hair flapping, gloved hands balled to fists, stayed one gob behind.

I slowed, passing the topless bar, and gazed distractedly at the drawings on the mimeographed flyers taped to the stuccoed walls of the windowless building.

As I turned the corner, the door opened and a goddess stepped out as though off of one of the posters, her red hair heaped in a hive. She wore a tight top and black stretch pants and I halted inches from her breasts.

"Whoa. Watch it there, kid," she winked.

The bar was not open yet and she must have been helping the owner set up. She gave Alex a look and walked on.

"Check that ass," he remarked.

"Alex, Nicholas," someone called our name from across the street.

Father Myron. A thin, bespeckled man with a motherly disposition, Father Myron was respected. When he crossed the street, cars stopped to let him pass.

"No place for a lemonade stand," he said to us, gesturing at the bar.

"We're on our way to the park for a frog."

"For Pietro."

"Now, no firecrackers, boys," he admonished.

"Oh, Mrs. Matejko," he waved to an old woman hobbling across the street on a walker.

A circle of poplars guarded the entrance to the park, an oasis pulsing with hidden creatures: squirrels, raccoons, possums, ducks, even a few heart-pounding foxes.

We were approaching the pond, our urban version of what we had in the Catskills, walking down the middle of the road when a red Mustang loomed from around the corner and I recognized Sammy Cochon and Billy the T, who lived on the next block. As the car roared by, Alex shouted:

"Assholes!"

I dropped my head into my hands. This was no time to die. We were on a mission; we had a frog to catch; I had to study my Latin declensions. Alex, meanwhile, seemed determined to reform his image.

The Mustang stopped. Behind us, I heard doors clicking open, banging shut, sharp-toed boots with taps drumsticks on the macadam, and before we could tear off, four of the toughest punks in town were blocking our way.

Sammy, guinea-Teed and toned from working out at Greg's Gym, leaned into Alex, who didn't pull away.

"Pussies," Alex muttered.

I saw then there were two options open before us: either negotiation or death.

"Have you heard about the giant frogs? Yeah, I'm not kidding. Bigger than your car. That's what we're going to check out."

"Fuck you."

As a final maneuver, I began screaming like a grandmother on fire, like Mrs. Obolonsky the morning her husband dropped dead during communion, which bought us a few seconds while I tried imagining the next step, when Officer Mike emerged from the bushes on the side of the road, where he'd probably been bopping some girl from the high school. His tie was loose and his blue shirt unbuttoned.

Officer Mike was famous for overreacting.

"Hello, Sammy. Boys. What's this, a revival meeting? Here to praise the Lord?"

Relieved by how suddenly our situations had reversed, I watched Sammy bury his hands so deep in his pockets they threatened to slip out near his ankles.

Mike's sleeves were rolled up, his face, white as a boiled chicken breast, glistened, and I thought I noticed lipstick on his chin.

Trapped, the four hoods swapped looks and you could feel the idea of jumping the cop flicker on the grid.

"Ever see angels praising the Lord?" Mike tilted his head back, his sensitive nose twitching like a rabbit's.

"No, sir," I answered.

"It's a brilliant sight. Oh, you'll enjoy this."

He turned to the culprits. His fat mouth flattened into a grin.

"Knees, boys."

"Kidding?"

"Knees. While you still got 'em. You, Sammy."

Everyone knew about Mike losing his temper, pulping people who'd pissed him off. He was the one cop kids were freaked by, thanks to rumors of bones broken, noses splayed, eyes tattooed, drugs stolen, and the power of a bad press had never been more evident.

After the four had dropped to their knees, Mike yanked out his nightstick and, holding it between his legs like an erection, he made each of the kids edge up to him and put their mouths on it.

"Suck it, boys. Good."

Finally satisfied, he dismissed us, his necessary audience, and we headed home without our frog.

On the way back, Alex took out his cigarettes and offered me one. I stopped and held it between my fingers and brought it up to my nose before finally planting it between my lips and letting him ignite it with a lighter that reeked of gasoline. He snickered at my coughing while I squinted through the smoke, hoping none of my mother's friends happened by. Three puffs were all I could manage while Alex assured me that, before long, I'd be begging for more.

I, meanwhile, couldn't put that album I'd glimpsed at Black Pond out of my mind. What were those photographs? How did God look behind the clouds? Why did Mrs. Kruk have them? Stained glass and icons in an age of 70mm movies and television weren't very convincing. Did God smile? How big was He? Sometimes I thought it would be wonderful if God was small, so tiny as to be nearly invisible. I imagined Him the size of a pen cap, dressed in chinos and topsiders, with a green plaid shirt, waving an umbrella that was actually the wand containing His power. He had only to aim, say the word, and we got: earthquakes, snow, love, miracles, the armadillo.

I kept asking Alex about the pictures until he finally agreed to bring out the album, warning me I'd be disappointed. It was a December Saturday. We were in the Kruk's kitchen. Snow had fallen the night before, giving the world a fine festive feel. Had I been God, I would have chosen just such a moment to show myself.

Alex carried in the book as though it were a telephone directory. As he set it down I looked at his profile and saw his mother in the thick lips, green eyes, and high forehead. Only the hooked nose was Lev's.

The album was a padded blue leatherette.

"Open it," he said.

I flung back the cover and my heart sank. Inside were hundreds of postcards depicting the Virgin Mary in a score of poses.

"Gotto," I read on the back of the card.

He flipped the page. "And that's one of my favorites"

I looked at the elongated Madonna swathed in a velvety green then turned it over to find a caption with another strange name: El Greco.

The names meant nothing to me. I shut my eyes to control my disappointment. Alex commented:

"What did you think? Mother's right, in a way. Great artists. Close as we'll get."

"How'd you know?"

"Gotta keep up, gumba." Then he added: "I've got something a lot better."

I had removed my glasses and was staring, blind and bored, at the blurred white world outside. Why had Ada teased me? I felt cheated. I decided it had to be a mistake: Alex didn't know. He didn't know where the real album was, so he had brought out this poor thing instead. Or maybe he did, but he didn't want me in on the secret. No, it pleased me more to imagine that he was not in on it—that Ada kept the album hidden from him. One day she would show me. Because I felt a curious intimacy with his mother and believed that in certain situations she might choose me over Alex. Who knows the source of my cheek? In the meantime, I'd pretend to be satisfied and behave as though the quiz were over. And I was impressed by Alex's new expertise: it seemed his enthusiasms weren't contained by his collections or his gloves, and that his compulsive personality was capable of curious things.

Alex came back with a magazine in his hand. That was how I became acquainted with *Playboy*.

My eyes widened as we explored the photographs whose colors already seemed faded. So this was what lay beneath all those robes! No wonder women hid themselves so artfully. Seeing the pictures for the first time, I reacted with a mix of shame, embarrassment, curiosity, and desire. Alex, on the other hand, seemed to have none of the first three. His response was a combination of desire and I could only call it awe. His hands trembled as he turned the pages. I grew impatient quickly and wanted to move on to the next picture, but he said:

"Wait, man. Look at that, look at that."

His eyes were glassy and his breathing shallow. Judging by his response, it's a wonder men weren't running through the streets, dragging women by the hair. And Ada—did she look like these women beneath her bathing suit?

The third or fourth time we met to examine still another journal, Alex furthered my education by pulling down his zipper and taking out his penis, which was filled with enthusiasm for the latest object of our attention.

"What? Never seen the dolphin flog?"

I shrugged. My own incipient response had been aborted by the public nature of the examination. I had by then had wet dreams but had not yet discovered how easy it was to recreate them in daylight.

"You haven't, have you?" He grinned. Then: "Come on, let's see it."

"What?"

"Goldfish, pal, show us your goldfish."

His own, which he coddled shamelessly in a loose fist, looked tuberous and knobby and I felt no desire to spill into his aquarium, but the fear of being ridiculed for my inexperience was more powerful than any inhibitions I might have internalized from who knows where? This was a good decade before the first sex education courses gave adolescents a window onto their own reactions and I don't believe I'd ever heard any adult make a single reference to sex. Certainly not my father or mother, certainly not the nuns. The closest I'd come to stumbling upon the mystery before had been by passing the go-go bar downtown where my reaction to the word topless was, if truth be told, much more full of incomprehension than leering.

"Go on," he urged me, rubbing a wet nose with the back of his other hand.

And slowly I unzipped my pants.

"Let's see."

Slipping my fingers like tweezers into my boxers, I emerged with a sorry specimen that lay there unresponsive as a shucked shrimp.

"Do this," Alex said, sliding the foreskin back. After a few pulls, his once more grew red and swollen. Again his eyes glazed and he looked away from me and at the picture; then his gaze went inward while has hand picked up speed and his breathing deepened and suddenly there was a wild twitching below and a geyser of white lava flying through the air and onto the bare floor of his small cluttered room with the animal skulls and the shells and the odd red rocks close around us, and he gave himself a last squeeze and shut his eyes.

By the time he returned, I'd zipped myself up, closed the magazine, and was sitting awkwardly on the edge of his bed.

He looked at me with calm bemusement.

"You've never done it?"

If his voice had been anything other than tender I might have denied it, might have claimed I simply hadn't been in the mood—but there was no mockery in him. He seemed glad to be my teacher, initiating me ever deeper into the ways of the world. His cheeks were red as though he'd run the six hundred.

I shook my head.

"Here," he said, pushing the magazine to me.

When I didn't respond, he said:

"Take it with you. Look at it in the bathroom. That's the place for this. Don't worry, everybody does it."

I didn't want to argue with him so I accepted his gift and over the next days I found the time and the place for a more private and prolonged exploration of cause and effect, and before long I too had mastered this singular masculine art about which so many had for centuries raised such a fuss and which our age finally turned into a project for health class.

Yet the force that Alex learned to unleash was one he never came to control, and I wonder how many of his subsequent problems were seeded in those earliest searches and seizures.

3

Love too is a type of disappearing sickness, which was something we discovered thanks to Paul.

Eldest sons grow big, their flesh a sheathe against the world's expectations. Paul's shoulders were broad as an upside-down canoe, capable of floating any number of passengers. He sported an athlete's buzz cut and dressed like a jock, though I knew from Alex that, despite his success on the football team, off the field he kept to himself. Not even the most rigorous work-outs, however, seemed capable of draining Paul's rage. Anger backlit his black eyes, which flickered like an oil spill on fire.

In Paul's junior year the police cruiser began to seem like the Kruk's private cab. He was brought home for staying out past curfew, trying to buy alcohol, throwing stones at a train. He was caught breaking windows in an abandoned house near the hospital, spray painting graffiti on the side of a bus, fighting in school, setting off firecrackers in the boy's room. He was suspended. If he got in trouble again, Ada was told, he would be expelled.

My father, who paid for medical school by working more jobs

than I could keep track of, was running the register at the local bodega when he caught Paul slipping a magazine under his shirt. He made the boy wait for him while he closed the store. Then he brought him home. He rang the bell and waited for Ada to appear. Viktor, who'd been asleep, stood in the light, blinking like a bat stunned by the sun.

Father knew about Viktor.

"Where's Ada?" he asked firmly.

"She's at the restaurant."

"Which one?"

"The diner."

Gripping a glum Paul by the collar of his denim jacket, Father set off.

They walked in silence. Had his captor been anyone but Father, there would have been a fight. Father, meanwhile, saw such missions as part of his ministry. Walking to the restaurant, he whistled his beloved Mozart, waving to his friends in the stores along the way.

Ada was standing outside, smoking a cigarette, when she saw her son moving toward her like the prow of a ship.

Seeing Father, she dropped her cigarette and buttoned her blouse higher.

She couldn't look at her Paul. Blindly she extended her hand and slapped him.

"What's he done, Peter?"

"I caught him stealing."

"I was not stealing."

"The criminal will deny even his own mother. I'm sorry, Ada. But I wanted you to know. I don't want him to go to jail."

"Thank you, Peter. How is Slava?"

"Always busy with some church committee. And the house." But he didn't want to underscore the obvious. He was a modest man, who saw Ada's pain.

"What should I do with him?"

Father thought a minute. "You should let him work with me at the store."

"I'll never work with you," Paul hissed.

"Ok. Nobody will force you. But you should get a job."

"I have to go back," Ada said. "Thank you for not calling the police, Peter."

What no one anticipated was the aphrodisiac power Paul's criminal status exercised over the Florentina sisters.

In the sixties, on its way to the suburbs, divorce also visited our neighborhood. The first two floors of the Kruk's house had until recently been occupied by Mr. and Mrs. Florentina, Italian immigrants who'd named their five daughters for the boroughs of New York. Soon after Lev left Ada, Jingles Florentina—he was called Jingles because of his over-reliance on his bicycle bell—abandoned his wife Beatrice and their five daughters. His departure devastated the girls. Beatrice, on the other hand, told Ada that personally she was thrilled.

All five of the boroughs were luscious. Through a hole in the floor of their bathroom, the Kruk boys had watched the girls grow up, showering in a peep show fine as any the boys might have paid money for in New York. Bronx was slight, with reddish-brown hair, and by fourteen she'd been accepted by a dancing academy downtown. Brooklyn, a brunette, was loud, gum-chewing, and always glad to meet a new boy. She dropped out of school to work in a travel agency, eventually marrying the boss. Queens, also a brunette, was bookish, destined for the library. Ai, as they nicknamed the Island, had a large nose and breasts she called her "silly machines" because of the way they made men react. She was wise to herself, though, and to everyone else, especially her youngest sister, Hattie.

Paul's age, Manhattan was the one unlikely blond in that brood, standing out like a Monroe among the Maui. The hair had once been black, of course, and she was layered in a dusky down along her neck and under her ears like a shadow of fur. Surrounded by such savvy sisters, she couldn't help being conscious of the magnetic power of hair flips and pouts. She tried containing her flirtatious impulses, without success. Love comes in at the eye: the chemistry of sight and response conditioned both Hattie and the men she attracted as absolutely as the hormonal transmissions between humans and mosquitoes.

Three of us fell in love with Manhattan at the same time, but here Paul had us beat. The trouble he'd gotten into had given him a certain cachet in the neighborhood. People knew who he was; some even feared him. What finally won her, though, was the episode with the wolf.

The air that August afternoon was soaked with summer smells: gasoline and ripe grapes, sweat, pizza, and seasonal decay. We were sitting out on the stoop when Hattie, wearing an orange halter, rushed past us and up the stairs. Paul whistled. Hattie whirled around:

"Pretty good, but you wanna see *my* wolf?"

We didn't hesitate.

She led us into the bedroom where blue floral wallpaper peeled like bark and was held in place with pins and thumb tacks. There was a photo of Paul McCartney on the dresser, a stack of *Teen* magazines, a .45 record player inside a tan burlap suitcase, and, on the pink chenille spread covering the bed, a wolf cub, its long tongue swabbing its teeth like a wet pink towel.

Hattie hovered above it, letting her blond hair waterfall over her shoulders. Paul gaped at her face, which eclipsed even the peculiar sight of the wolf. Her features were so fine, more sweepingly Irish than Mediterranean, an up-curved nose, and olive eyes. Her loose shorts flashed tawny thighs. She was brown all over from sunbathing on the roof. Alex, who was wearing his suede gloves, and I both watched him watching her. We were learning the signals.

"Where'd you get it?"

"I'll never tell."

"Your mother gonna let you keep it?"

Hattie smiled.

She pulled out a box of liver treats, the cub tongued from her hand.

I later learned the animal had been stolen from a small private zoo in the suburbs by a boy who wanted Hattie's attention, which I don't think he received.

She took it for walks in the neighborhood where it had a stimulating effect. Seeing the wolf startled people into a heightened sense of the moment. They took to it. The butcher tossed it scraps of raw burger, my father's friend at the bodega slipped it Armour hot dogs. Hattie walking the wolf on a pink leash gave the place glamour. Even Pietro was impressed. He swept off his hat, bowed deeply, and said: "An honor to make your acquaintance, Mr. Houston." Only the Spinner seemed scared of it—maybe it reminded him of Siberian episodes best forgotten.

Eventually the wolf escaped, becoming the subject of considerable media attention: For a few days the neighborhood watched itself on the news while Hattie was interviewed by a man who wore more make-up than Ada. It was then that Paul and Hattie drew close. He became her hired gun. He spent hours helping her search for the cub; they cut school, stayed out late. Mrs. Florentina visited Adriana to complain that the kids were going too far, but the business had become bigger than anything they could control. Newspapers loved the story; television cameras from Newark stalked the street, and a posse was assembled that eventually tracked down the cub to a lilac hedge in Warinenco Park where Officer Mike shot it without hesitation. Hattie asked for the body but the county sheriff said she should be grateful he didn't arrest her for receiving stolen property.

She consoled herself by taking Paul into her bed. He became her wolf, something wild and feral that could guard her in this world. Paul told Alex the day after it happened and Alex quickly relayed the news to me. He didn't say it crudely, didn't brag, but it changed Paul, dulling some of his edge. His eyes, normally nervous and darting, slowed until he could really see you, take you in.

Hattie was a haven for Paul. Their passion was like a mobile home liberating them from the terrain of tenements and limp dreams. They enlarged each other, and each seemed better for the other's sympathy. Hattie too relaxed, easing herself more fully into the world.

Alex benefited indirectly—Hattie practically lived in their room. She was physical, a toucher, always putting her hands on Alex's shoulder when she talked to him, or mussing his hair, unaware how he trembled under her stroke or the way his eyes revisited her breasts as though they were a tourist attraction. In an exuberant mood she would hug him as Ada never did—for some reason Ada kept a distance from her sons physically: maybe they reminded her of Lev, or other ghosts. An invisible wall had arisen between her and her sons, yet her physical coldness was strange given how much she thought about them and how sexual she was. Or perhaps that was it—she was frightened by the unpredictable chemistry of touch.

Once Alex and Hattie were sitting in the kitchen together when Ada returned from work early. Alex could never keep her schedule straight. Paul was at the garage but Ada was pleased to see Hattie. The two blondes seemed fond of each other.

After asking about her mother and sisters, Ada blurted out:

"I have a photograph of Jesus. Have I showed you?"

Hattie shook her head.

Adriana went to her room and came back with the same frayed postcard I'd studied the previous summer.

Hattie giggled.

"That's a drawing, Mrs. Kruk."

"I know," Adriana sighed, sitting down in the chair.

Alex, again embarrassed by his mother, stood up and excused himself.

"No, Alex, I want you to hear this. Get me some water, dear. Thank you."

Then she turned to Hattie, who plucked at her hair.

"We're both blond, Mrs. K.," she said.

"I was once in love with a poet named Anton," Ada said, staring intensely at the girl. Anton was the poet who lived in England and whose visit had already been postponed twice without explanation.

Alex seethed—here was the old world he was learning to hate slipping into the room again. He felt the tribe of hungry ghosts surrounding him with long chalk bodies. He watched as they hauled Hattie onto a boat and carried her off into the fog, but when he tried to speak his mother's glares silenced him. Her needs paralyzed him.

"Anton lived as a guest in a large house owned by a rich old woman. I don't think it was as big as the house your mother worked in, but it was in the city. There was a harp and a grand piano in the parlor. Tapestries hung from the walls. The old woman lived alone, except for her servants and Anton. His room was in the attic. When the servant opened the door for me I could smell the garlic, and when she put a hand on my arm I swear she left a piece of her skin there. I remember going up the stone stairs to Anton's room. Long before getting there, I'd smell smoke. It was Anton who taught me to smoke. He smoked everything: cigarettes, pipes, cigarillos. He wanted to try opium but he couldn't get any. Have you ever tried opium, dear?"

Hattie shook her head, giggling.

"He wrote and wrote. He knew English very well. He recited poems he had translated. His fingers were long as the legs of a spider. He'd point to a volcano of pages on the floor—you could practically see the orange smoke rising—and say ten thousand sheets had gone to make the one he held in his hands. 'How will anybody know,' I asked. 'They shouldn't care. It's my business.' 'But why do you do it? Everything will just be thrown away,' I said. He said, 'because a few words might not be thrown away, if they're the right ones.' He was trying to find the right words. He said they would carry him into the future. He said the world didn't care about tears or blood. The world would count bodies and say a number: eight million. Eight million people died here. This would go down in history books. And children would ask: 'where? Where did eight million people die?' Teacher points to a dot on the globe: 'there.' Child: 'Lotta people for one dot. How'd they fit?' If even part of that dot has a name, a face, a mother—if just one of those eight million ever walked a dog or spilled his coffee hurrying to work, then maybe so did the remaining eight million. He gave me this. He said: 'It's the world's only photograph of Jesus.' We laughed too. I'm sorry you never met him."

"That's a funny story," said Hattie, still playing with her hair. "I gotta go find Paul."

Hattie drew a map of North America across the back of Paul's hand. His knuckles were the ragged edges of the Arctic Circle. "I give the world the back of my hand," he crowed to Alex and me.

Hattie said part of the reason she liked him was because he was both familiar and strange. They'd grown up as neighbors yet at the same time he was from a place that was off the charts, a country you won't find on any map.

One muggy August afternoon, Hattie came hunting for Paul, who'd gone to work at the garage. She asked Alex if he wanted to sit on the roof and get some sun. The broiled tar was sticky in places. Alex stared as she peeled off her orange top and shorts, revealing a washed-out green bikini. She stretched out her red towel and asked him to rub lotion on her. Start with my feet, she said, lying on her stomach, and he did, moving up her ankles and the backs of her knees. From the street drifted voices and car sounds and an occasional plane passed overhead. She rolled on her back, eyes closed. He moved his hand down her shoulders and over the tops of her breasts. When he lingered she said, 'Hey, keep it movin' buster,' and he worked his way down slowly, wishing she would grow longer so he would never finish. He rose, dizzy from coconut oil, and leaned against the chimney and stared out at the squares of the houses sprawling cacophonously all the way to the steely ocean. He thought he knew the world, this wild place of relentless elbowing and competition, moody and arbitrary and tending toward violence, and he wondered how his small self would stand up to it. But now as he listened to the plane, his eyes half-closed, and his heart beating hard, he knew that Hattie, or someone like her, was the secret, the soft flesh and the invisible energies of love would pull him through, and he thanked his brother for this gift of an afternoon. He had learned another way of disappearing. And he was quick to share news of his good fortune with me.

And yet it did not end well. Hattie knew she would always fall in love with men who would leave: that was her destiny. Look at her father. Her wolf. And because she knew that some day Paul too would split, she decided to beat him to it by being one of only two people from the neighborhood to go away to school. The other, of course, was me, though by then we had moved to Fort Hills.

4

Of course, the most dramatic disappearing act in the Kruk family was Lev's.

Before telling that story I should point out that what I know about the Kruks' early years in this country I've sutured together from fragments offered by Ada, Alex, and even my parents, while using the adhesive of imagination whenever the pieces seemed too jagged to cohere: less the facts than the feel of things.

They had not always been seen as pariahs by the community. Like my parents, the Kruks arrived at Ellis Island early in 1950, at a time when American cities were starting to bulk up. All hustle and energy, recently decommissioned soldiers put their training to use spawning new businesses: Spectacular Buicks and Chryslers cruised the confident streets. Meanwhile, a virus infected the imagination of postwar architects and urban planners, and for the next decade public buildings appeared to have been modeled on mausoleums, as though the millions of war dead huddled in the hallways of the unconscious, clamoring to be honored.

Ada had read about Greenwich Village and Wall Street and Fifth Avenue, but nothing had prepared her for the seizure that is New York. She stepped out into a torrent of silks and suits, black shoes and high heels, sweeping her along until the tributaries bled into one roaring rapid pulling her under while she scanned for a dock. Where was the Opera House? The school at which her mother had taught?

One night she dreamed she'd fallen asleep in a field of stones and was awakened by the sound of footsteps. She opened her eyes on a vision: a golden spiral stairway, like a double helix etched in light, had dropped out of the sky. On it an endless stream of angels with skulls stencilled on their wings jogged up and down like commuters on the escalator at Grand Central. She awoke refreshed, feeling that perhaps God was willing to follow her even to this unfathomable place. She subsequently began going out to places that also overwhelmed her, but in different ways: visiting the Metropolitan Museum, she could not believe the ardor gathered under one roof, nor could she grasp the scale of the operation; yet she went regularly, always stopping at the gift shop to buy more postcards of the Madonna, to whom she often prayed.

As soon as possible the Kruks moved to a smaller city in northern New Jersey.

There, the list of things bewildering Adriana about America included front lawns, doctors, cars, the telephone, the natives' difficulties with consonants, speed, and the worship of success. After all, she'd come from a place where until recently friends had lived within walking distance and visitors appeared unannounced, though slowly. Back yards, meanwhile, were for growing vegetables. Moreover, nobody from her borderland believed any single language could ever convey all one's needs or say the world in its fullness. Most importantly, perhaps, in place of success, failure was worshipped. What is Christianity, a religion insisting the last shall be first, and the first last, if not the triumph of failure?

But as she found her bearings she learned to trust her new home, and she came to love the crowded downtown areas, the great bazaars of Woolworth's and Gimbel's and Daffy Dan's, where the attending noise and energy slowly erased one's self. Mass production seemed a miracle. Thanks to the radio, she had access to the greatest music in the world, as well as to news from everywhere.

The fact that half her fellow citizens in America didn't vote seemed to Adriana a good sign, while her husband took it as proof that the population had been rendered passive by technologies he viewed as the ruling elite's wittiest weapon yet in the eternal war between those who worked and those who played. Adriana left politics to Lev. She expected to concentrate on home and the refreshments of culture, and she thanked God for a haven in which to recover from a Europe where neighbors sharpened knives against each other, revenge their sustaining force.

In the new world, Lev became a Teamster, a union man, and for a while he believed the blank page of the future crackled at the prospect of his unfolding destiny. Yet the transition from revolutionary to lathe operator on an assembly line insulted his imagination, which had cast him more romantically, as a consul or a spy. He knew it was temporary; even so, he was hurt he'd not been recognized for all that he was. Couldn't they see how much energy and desire he had? One atom unleashed could level a city. Imagine what he might do if conditions were right.

But somehow they never were. It was hard to say why—there was something subtle, something sly about America that eluded him. And slowly his body grew tense and stiff as a crab under siege.

Many of his friends adapted with ease. They took menial jobs gladly. They enrolled in night schools and, over time, earned degrees and entered the professions. They became doctors, dentists, lawyers, and later, computer operators; or, they worked as brewers, dock workers, truck drivers, and plant managers. Watching them recreate themselves was painful for Lev. He wondered what there was inside him: what block, what lock, what bar that kept him from making the switch? He blamed the handful of books he'd read as a young man, which convinced him life only had value experienced at a certain level of possibility. He hungered for that sense of infinite promise. If only we can hope to climb ever upward, we have our reason for moving. It wasn't the ladder of material success he schemed to scale—Lev wanted something more boyish: to search for a grail that would give meaning to everything that came before. Without it, the deserts of dailiness weren't worth the trouble and the past was a trousseau of dust.

The pressure of Alex's illness (that disappearing sickness, which no one in the family would disavow) along with Lev's congenital loneliness and the distaste he felt for his job, inclined Lev to rages. The soccer field was only one of the places he unleashed his anger, deliberately pouring it into Paul. The kid needed toughening. How else could he teach him the lessons of the world?

America was soft on its young. They knew nothing of life. He wanted Paul powerful, his muscles pure verb. He wanted his anger to learn how to sing.

Ada understood: He lacked the courage to let his sons love him even in failure. At the same time she saw how trapped her husband was by his circumstances, how he could not help believing that in this society everyone was relentlessly measuring everyone else, and it was clear that he was not measuring up.

What nobody recognized was that Lev's fear of failure would reemerge in his sons as a willful courtship of the very thing from which he fled.

Their kitchen seemed no bigger than a walk-in closet, yet it held not only a refrigerator that hummed like a prop plane, a double sink, and a Sears range, but also a large, claw-footed bathtub that Lev had topped with a slab of plywood. Covered with a red and white oilcloth, it served the Kruks for a table. The room was spotless: floor, sink, and walls appeared fresh-scrubbed; but for the cracked bottom pane, the window might have been made of pressed air.

Ada always began preparations for dinner immediately after breakfast, as though fearing that if she left the kitchen for a minute, the food might not be there when she returned. This morning, she stood at the sink chopping onions, adding them to the borscht simmering on the spotless stove. A fine net of sweat bubbled up over her high-cheeked face. She held a spoon in one hand and a sponge in the left.

Lev had decided not to go in to work. He'd called the main

office a few minutes before and said he was sick. The day loomed like a threat. She hated it when he stayed home.

He appeared absorbed by the paper but he turned the pages too quickly. He rubbed his neck, where the guilt had lodged while the traffic outside reproached him for responsibilities slighted, and the tension in the room was so great that Ada, normally nimble with a knife, knicked her finger not once but twice. Both times she'd suppressed a yelp. The boys had gone off to school a few minutes before.

"You'll lose your job," she finally said, regretting it immediately.

That was enough.

"What?" he screamed, the hair trigger pulled. He threw down the newspaper and stomped over to the stove.

"What are you saying?"

His skin looked pink as her beet-stained hands. She could feel his coffee breath on her neck.

"I should throw you out into the street! I work. Six days a week I work. A man needs a break."

Her being contracted, concentrated.

"You pretend you have work to do. What you do in a day I could do in an hour," he snarled.

Finally, refusing silence, she whirled, knife in hand, and lashed back:

"You whining little man. Look at Ihor or Edward. They hide from their jobs? They do what they have to," she hissed.

It was too much and Lev, for the second time that morning, raised his hand.

At night, after the boys had gone to bed, it was different.

The bedroom had the cultivated feel of a temple, a sacred place. Ada had done what she could to brighten it with embroidered curtains and an intricately stitched hand-made towel thrown across the dresser that she'd bought from Mrs. Dumka at the church bazaar.

The double bed was just large enough for the couple and, after feuding, they curled up together as though all they'd exchanged over the course of the day had been blown kisses. Soon Lev's hand found her breast and she yielded with a sigh.

The night ended with her kissing him and telling him how much she loved him. During the war it was Lev who'd protected her. It was Lev who did what they needed to do to get to America. It was Lev who'd found this apartment in which they finally had their own bedroom—just as she'd had back home in her father's house. Lev had given her some stability in a world that cared less about her than the weather.

Blinds knocked the sill in the breeze.

For some years, Alex was her great consolation. He was his mother's darling and his sickness only intensified her reason for being. She lavished him with looks and kisses like the feathery licks of a bird-dog.

In return, he was enchanted by Adriana's dead. As a child, Alex saw them as vividly as she did—which puzzled her, since he'd never known his aunts or uncles alive. He'd seen them only as they appeared in the cheaply framed photographs covering every flat space in the place not already occupied by an ashtray. Yet whenever Nina, for instance, appeared, Alex clapped his hands, smiled, and pointed. Ada took solace from this confirmation of her visions. Death bound them from the start. His interest in her ghosts kept them alive for her.

As he grew, his powers faded, though Ada coaxed both sons, saying: "Look, there's your aunt." Or: "Listen, the wind is calling your brother's name." Half of it was a deliberate poetry on her part, as she sought to domesticate the weird world exploding around her. In cities, the trees were dying and she feared one day the sky itself would be a bubble of plastic. But no matter what she did, she felt her sons growing strange to her, and her home invaded by forces almost as destructive as those she faced during the war. While she wasn't oblivious to the wonder of television, for years she refused to allow one in the house. No matter how her sons protested, she stayed firm. There were enough dead to keep Alex and Paul company for a lifetime. The uncontainable spirits of aunts and uncles fluttered among them like moths; moreover, trees and flowers boasted their own avatars eager to connect with the human. Television might distract them, prevent them from learning how to tune to the frequency of the past—and without that continuity, who would they be? Wraiths of appetite and the whims of the moment.

As the dead slowly faded from the picture, what took their place was America. How could it not? Who could avoid it? The killing of the Kennedys—by the mob, Lev believed; the civil rights' marches, all those spoiled lives; the war in Vietnam; the space launches: it appeared every important event in the world in that period happened either in America or because of it. If it didn't happen here, it may as well not have happened at all.

Unfortunately, Ada carried two decades of memories from another country, full of other buildings and other people, all of which had been real as the ones surrounding her now; they superimposed themselves onto the faces she saw in the streets, so she had to stop herself from waving to a man she thought she recognized, a former classmate, a second cousin who once lived around the corner on whom she'd had a crush and who quite possibly still lived there, in a city on the other side of the world where life continued without her, and where even at this moment someone she'd known in short pants may well have been thinking of her.

The first evening Lev didn't come home from work Ada stayed up all night, pacing madly, smoking cigarettes. In the morning, after the boys left for school, she went down and explained her dilemma to Mrs. Florentina, who immediately called the police. Ada had a premonition he'd been hit by a green newspaper delivery truck. The disappearing sickness, she thought to herself. But there had been no reports of any incidents. Finally she walked down to the plant, where she was told Lev had been fine when he left the day before, but they didn't expect him back until later that afternoon—he'd asked to work second shift for the rest of that week.

She returned home and waited. In the meantime, she made pirohy. Her sons found her sweating in the kitchen, a babushka wrapped around her hair, and a pyramid of cigarettes in the ashtray. They asked when Lev would be home. Ada ignored them and went on cooking. By six, mad with worry, she sent Paul out to the plant. He returned with a confused look on his face and said he'd been told that his father was there but that he didn't want to see him.

That could mean only one thing. Too overwhelming. Ada began singing snatches of half-remembered songs. *Keep my face under control. Breathe*. Paul fought his own panic and tried calming his mother, but she pushed him away and told both boys to go to their rooms.

"Homework," she said.

She went downstairs to share her suspicions with Mrs. Florentina. She broke down and sobbed. Who would believe that her husband might leave them after everything they'd already been through?

"Why you think he leave? How you know?" Beatrice asked sensibly.

"I just know, I just know," Ada screamed. "He's a man. He has no feelings."

Finally Mrs. Florentina convinced her to drink a little whiskey and she calmed down. Toward dawn she fell asleep for an hour. Then she awoke and got her sons up and, ignoring their questions, sent them off to school.

She was determined to confront Lev. That afternoon she didn't wait for the boys to come home. She dressed herself in her Sunday clothes, put on perfume and lipstick, and took herself down to the factory. It was a cool October day; leaves cluttered the gutters. An orange sun painted the streets. She remembered how much she'd once loved autumn and she pulled her coat tight against the breeze.

There he was, walking beside a young woman with broad shoulders, black velvet shoes, red lips. Not what she'd expected. When he saw Ada he stopped. Without taking his eyes off his wife, he said something to the girl, who immediately turned and headed in the other direction. He walked on alone. He was wearing the same chocolate suit, as well as the ubiquitous cap he had on when he stepped out of the house two days ago. She'd washed and ironed the shirt herself. As he drew nearer, Ada saw that his face was closed and his eyes shielded.

She glared, hoping the rage pouring from her would lash him with its fiery tail, hurtle him to the ground, but he just walked up and looked at her and didn't say anything while his thin lips strained out a smile.

And suddenly her anger left her. She felt her body again seized by sobs and she threw herself at his chest. He held her while she wept and when she looked up she saw his face had softened a little. Maybe there was still hope.

"Come home," she said,

He shook his head.

Then she became angry again. She pushed him away, glaring, her green eyes hurling fire.

"Who cared for you all these years? Held you, nursed you, gave you children? How can you do this?" she screamed.

"Ada, the people," he said. Several of his coworkers had stopped a few feet away and were watching the drama. Ada ignored them. She felt a great tectonic shift inside her, a sense of things breaking up. How could the man who'd protected her become her enemy? A train of dark thoughts roared through her head. She wanted to cut her husband to pieces with her nails and squeeze his heart in her fist. What would she do now?

Nina's spirit sang in Adriana's ear. She heard the song clearly. It was one her mother loved, about crickets and calm waters, and it reassured her. It helped to know her sister's ghost was still with her. Nina whispered in her ear, telling her that this would pass, that the Lord was watching over her, even when she didn't think he was.

After a long while Lev pulled away from her grasp. He stared at her red eyes and his own seemed to cloud over. For a second, she had hope—he would say something, change his mind, everything would be all right. But he simply stepped back and walked around her. Years of communion and certainty, of love and companionship, turned to ash.

The next weeks were the worst in Ada's life. Not even the death of her parents matched this betrayal. Day after day Ada kept expecting he would realize what he'd done and return to them. Surely the madness was a toxic cloud that had settled over his heart that the sunlight of memory would burn away.

She lay in bed, listening to the surf breaking through the veins in her arms and her chest. She sucked down cigarette after cigarette, soothed by their poisons. Portents seemed everywhere: in the cracks on the ceiling, and in the random cries from the street. A voice on the radio said the word *tomorrow* and she suddenly felt certain the announcer was speaking about Lev's return. Tomorrow he would be back. Tomorrow was another country in which the landscape of today did not exist. Today and yesterday would all be erased by tomorrow as surely as the snow melted into the gutters after just one warm day. That was all it took, just one warm day.

She'd begun to convince herself when she thought about the boys, how hurt they were already, how much damage had been done, and she smoked some more.

Paul, whose battles with Lev had forged what he'd believed was a powerful bond, felt particularly stunned. At first the brothers stayed up late talking, trying to explain to each other what had happened, struggling above all to excuse their father. There was a reason he hadn't called or tried to see them. This was not their fault. As days turned to weeks, they ceased badgering their mother with questions. When their father visited, they didn't know how to reproach him. They felt anger but they couldn't speak it. Instead it would erupt unexpectedly. It was around this time Paul began getting into fights at school. During gym his classmates began avoiding him because he played so rough.

One day Alex answered the doorbell and there stood Lev. Alex stared silently at his new goatee.

"She's not here," he said finally, flexing his gloved fingers.

"Who is it?" Viktor, who'd recently moved in with them, called out.

"Nobody," Alex replied.

His father rubbed his beard as though sizing up his son, then he turned and walked away.

He didn't come again until the spring. This time he called ahead and arranged with Ada to see both boys. It was a Saturday, bright and windy, and he took them out in his red Buick to the Bronx Zoo, and as the three of them walked by the zebras and the giraffes, he tried talking to them as though nothing had happened.

"They used to call your mother the giraffe, you know."

They did their best to play along, but the flow of affection between them had ceased, replaced by dead air. All three were glad when the day was over and he was gone.

Ada was able to keep her sons from learning that Lev hadn't even asked for custody—not of course that she would have given it to him, but she would have liked knowing it was something he wanted. Lev, however, seemed satisfied with his new girl, and nothing else mattered.

After this, he simply slipped out of their lives. Occasionally one of the boys might get a card from him months late for a birthday, but by then it might have been signed by a stranger for all it meant to them.

Nina's spirit proved especially helpful during Ada's trials. Nina showed a confidence you didn't expect in a being who'd spent less than a day embodied, though Adriana had concluded that body and spirit relied on different chronometers, and little children often sported old souls. Over the weeks only Nina's assurances, along with her own prayers, calmed her and kept her from going mad.

Before the world, Ada appeared so composed that friends asked whether she wasn't secretly pleased Lev had gone.

"Is there someone else?" My mother asked.

"Only Jesus," Adriana assured her.

5

Had it been only Jesus consoling her, Ada might have struggled through this period. But her features seemed refined by suffering until she appeared as the transfigured Jeanne Moreau–like beauty I remember pecking at Black Pond, and it wasn't long before she discovered more palpable balms for her solitude.

She took a job as a waitress at the Italian restaurant where her neighbor, Beatrice Florentina, sometimes worked. Its owner, Ray Elba, watched as night after night, despite the year-round lure of Christmas lights in the windows and the plastic wreaths on the wall, his restaurant remained empty. He sat at a table in the back, away from the kitchen so his staff wouldn't think he was spying on them, sipping Chianti and picking his teeth and smelling his money rot along with the vegetables and the fish.

One June evening Adriana stood at her station near the swinging doors leading to the kitchen, joking with Elmira, Ray's sister, a burly girl with a dark mustache, whose fiancé seemed drifting toward trouble. In shadows, near trays of silverware, they mulled the sins of men and boys. And suddenly Ada felt grateful for a place to go, to see and be seen, where she could take the half-words swirling through her, the vowelless gnashing of the dead, and lay them out, incomprehensible and surely mistranslated, before another human being.

It was warm and rainy and the window fogged. The air conditioner had broken down the previous week and everyone was sweating. Inside the kitchen the two dishwashers tossed around a live chicken the cook fetched down from Ray's farm outside Princeton. The squawking echoed through the empty dining room. That night there were four patrons, a couple, and two single men. All but one looked so dour, Ray considered paying them to smile.

The sole friendly customer was a talkative and stocky older man who kept asking Ada to join him. "I'm working," she protested.

His name was Sammy, Samuel Robinwood. His crew-cut was the color of the aluminum fork while his round face flushed with wine. He entered wearing a cheap tan raincoat over a black wool jacket with a vaguely military cut and with the left sleeve pinned to the shoulder where the arm should have been. He sat erect and dignified, and his right hand alternately swallowed the wine glass and spun the spaghetti, deftly for a one-armed man.

"Time for my medication," he said to himself, motioning to Ada for more water. "The war," he mumbled.

The word had a magical effect on her: despite her experiences in refugee camps, she never thought of America in terms of the war. There was so little evidence of it around her—no shelled buildings or craters in the road.

When she returned she saw he'd laid out half a dozen colored bottles. Sensing her interest, Sammy explained what each of the medicines was for: prednisone for the joints, glycerin for the heart. Every organ had its own tablet. When she brought his check, he invited her to the movies.

She was flustered. She'd shrugged off countless passes but no one had ever asked her out on a date. She had her sons, her work, and her brother: enough. She was nearly forty years old.

How to respond? Say nothing. She walked away, and when he waved his check she asked Elmira if she'd take it for her.

"Why?"

Ada flexed forefinger to thumb: a talker. Elmira nodded.

And a one-armed man, how would that be? Everybody knows something different. What does a one-armed man know?

Am I still pretty, she wondered, looking into the mirror at the end of a shift, at graying hair, the soft, thick lips, seeing as though for the first time how much make-up she'd taken to applying: ever more violet to her lids, a brighter red to her mouth. These eyes had seen the Black Sea in a rage, and her home turned a pillar of salt.

She raked her fingers through the hair she planned to dye an even gaudier gold, and recalled lounging with Lev at Black Pond not long ago. Without him she had been miserable there, fending off the lecherous Semen, scared to estrange him because she needed friends.

But the next night Sammy was back, and the night after that, too.

Each time, he repeated his performance, undaunted by her blank stare.

His deep voice drowning Sinatra, Sammy asked why she wouldn't go out with him once, and she blushed, as though embarrassed someone at the other table might overhear—though of course the next table was empty.

What else is there for me, she argued with herself, except worrying about Alex and Paul, ghosts, and photos of ghosts.

Yes, she finally said, agreeing to meet him the next evening in front of the Liberty Theatre.

He gave her a quick salute, slipped neatly into the raincoat with the pinned-up sleeve, and walked out into the wet night. She stood in the doorway fingering her hair, watching him shuffle down the soft-lit, drizzly street.

Heading home after shopping the next afternoon, she saw a crowd marching down Broad Street. Most of the people were black. Leading them was a man shouting into a bull horn that garbled his words so Ada couldn't understand them. They were protesting something. She looked at the marchers' determined faces. They'd been dragged here too. Forced to leave home. Not unlike her. Even worse. Again she felt she had stepped into the middle of someone else's story: Gretel in Oz. Where did she belong? Would she ever find a plot line in the national narrative?

At the theater that night she was surprised when Sammy said he'd left his wallet behind, and would she mind paying? He'd reimburse her, *toutes de suite*—he used the French phrase, which he had learned in, of all places, France, and was in general given to salting his rambles with words that made her feel she was in the company of a worldly fellow. He passed on popcorn, opting instead for a coke. Watching the film, she sighed: no one would ever make a movie about her. No one on earth knew her story. She was startled out of herself though when, in the middle of *The Last of the Mohicans*, Sammy leaned over and clamped his hand to her breast. Ada didn't try to shake him off. On the contrary, she encouraged him. Many months had passed since a man had touched her. She'd forgotten everything. His one hand did the work of two, it seemed, and she let it.

After the film, she brought him home. Her conscience hissed at her as she crossed the threshold—but she was lonely, lonely. She'd had no relief in so long, no one to hold, no one to kiss, or be kissed by—in that other, essential way. Her boys were vessels into which she poured herself without receiving anything in return. Who dared tell her what was right, after all that had happened to her?

She tried to be quiet but Paul heard her come in. He woke up Alex and the two of them listened at the door as the anxious couple hurried into Ada's room.

She hesitated. I should send him home, she thought, looking at his large shadow in the doorway, watching him drop his coat on the floor, his one arm quickly undoing the buttons of his shirt, then reaching for her before she could decide anything. It was the arm, the one arm of the warrior that drew her close and held her, that made her submit with a wet, murky joy, even as she thought she heard noises in the hall, even as she wondered what the boys might think if they knew.

Which of course they did. There was no concealing the sounds of love caroling through the apartment that night.

What they heard haunted them like Adriana's ghosts.

Sammy's illnesses, his wounds, and his mortality made him a kind of border guard at the gates of the country she was most curious about. He foreshadowed what lay on the other side. She had fantasies of riding him so hard he'd die between her thighs. Her own thoughts frightened her, but she was incapable of regarding herself critically—the good work her parents had done in building her confidence as a girl. Wasn't sex called a little death? Yes, she'd drive this cheap small dear to collapse then nurse him back, and he would tell her what she needed to know. She remembered the sea and gathering chestnuts and the fabulous world of her childhood. She gave him her breasts and nibbled on the mushrooms of his ears.

While she might have had her own motives for getting together, he wasn't complaining. For nearly a year she made herself so available to Sammy he began feeling he had a harem of acrobatic houris at his call. She was his slave, his Salammbo, his O. She not only serviced him sexually, she fed him at the restaurant, tearing up his checks and having his meals deducted from her wages. Moreover, she had someone to talk to again. They spoke: she in broken English, he in the singular nasal staccato of northern Jersey. He'd been somebody, it turned out. He'd landed on the beach at Normandy. Later, he'd worked in the records department at City Hall. He knew the town, and people knew him. She felt strangers' eyes on her when they walked down the street together: they were her streets now.

He explained the world to her. That was something she still wanted from a man: someone to tell her why certain things happened—because it was a man's world, and only a man would know.

He told her about the different bureaus in City Hall, places where deeds were kept, where dogs were registered, and how the census was taken. He knew about real estate and taxes and permits and violations, and he told her that her restaurant was one of the cleanest in the city. He told her about ordinances and city council meetings, Memorial Day and the mayor. She had no idea the city was such a hive of busyness. A larger world loomed in her mind, distracting her from her own troubles.

She made him tell her about the war, about Normandy, the blood and the death, and this too relieved her. Talking about the war, she became animated and young, remembering herself as she had been, as one world was dying and the other a flicker in the imagination, a word on the tongues of strangers.

"Secret of America," he said, "is creation of value. What value do you have for others?"

"Then what good am I?" she mourned, drizzling her blondness into his sunken chest.

"Ah," he said, surprising even himself. "Better than you know. You remind me. We're born valuable. Only thing we need to do is one thing."

Her heart raced. It helped to hear this. Could she do it? Could she make herself matter?

"What's that?"

"Love our neighbors, babe. That's all." And he leaned over and mauled her breast.

"Here everything's possible," he said, "if you're willing to pay the piper. And the price isn't fixed, if you know how to bargain."

Sammy collected insects. In his apartment overlooking the harbor he had trays of beetles and test tubes of spiders and framed moths on the walls. Ada stared at them with horror and wonder. How formidable the flaking blue wings; how hideous the hairy mouths.

One evening he brought her a present. They were sitting in her kitchen around the bathtub, drinking tea with brandy.

Inside a special frame resembling a wooden shoe box with a glass lid was a creature unlike any she'd ever seen before. It was a thin, scaly black wand half the length of her arm, with bulging eyes that looked like orange berries glued to its tip.

"It's a Walking Stick," he said. "South American. Very rare."

She stared at the creepy bug that looked like a long tar candle with legs and eyes and wings, and she hoped it wouldn't return to life and break out of its frame.

As soon as he left, she slid it under her bed.

For a while she wanted to be with him all the time. In his company she felt safe and protected as she hadn't since Lev's departure. How could she be expected to handle so much alone?

She entrusted the boys to Viktor, who sometimes disappeared for days, leaving them to fend for themselves, to which they had no objections.

She started wanting Sammy fiercely. She imagined his hand raking the soft suede of her skin. Without him beside her, she had nightmares. She shot up in the middle of the night, perspiring, sheets damp, long yellow hair pasted to her neck, breathing heavily, and stared around the bedroom in the dark, at the furniture, which seemed startled to see her awake at that hour. "Mother!" she cried. She imagined the Walking Stick insect come alive, burst from its frame. She thought she saw it pressed to the wall, the orange eyes burning like embers. The brown dresser cowered in its corner; the night table shuddered. Ada sat in bed, head in her hands: Jesus was gone.

But what did she need Jesus for when there was a man beside her? An embrace, a kind word from human lips were so far more than promises.

At the restaurant she told Elmira:

"So late in life to find this out."

And yet something troubled her, too: guilt about the boys, or the sense that something was off, a core of humor missing. The laughter of the body that she remembered from her youth had been replaced by a sadness, and a liminal world hovered around every moment.

One evening, as she lay in his bed, lids sealed with fingers, she saw her mother standing in the kitchen of their old apartment. Her glasses were off and her eyes glittered as they had when she was young. She wore a pleated blue dress and looked as though she'd just returned from a date. She reached for her and her mother smiled and offered her a hand. Then she felt Sammy's palm on her knee and she turned to him with all the hunger of a lifetime.

He seemed to recognize it was temporary, that this waitress he'd scored, who was charged with more passion than anyone he'd known before, would eventually come to her senses—or leave them. Such intensity could not be sustained. This only made him more eager to prolong the connection. He used every resource. His own life had not been particularly easy: his father had worked in the mills of Lowell, Massachusetts, before taking a job at a brewery outside Newark. His mother had died when he was ten. The war had scarred him too, and not just by taking his arm, but by claiming the lives of both his brothers. He'd never been a joiner, and, having nothing to do with the VFW, he'd also kept the memories of his experiences to himself. Who wanted to know about it? Most of his colleagues at City Hall cared less about yesterday, and as for the younger generation, half an hour seemed like old times. Married for nearly a decade in the early fifties, he divorced his wife when he learned she was having an affair with a neighbor, and for the next ten years his only company had been an occasional hooker picked up in Newark. Mostly he'd devoted himself to his work and to his insect collecting. He hadn't realized how he longed for company until Ada. He knew almost nothing about this Ada's country, and its history enlarged his world—he too learned he wasn't the only one nursing wounds.

One night, after Ada had peeled off her clothes and stretched out across the red sheets of his small bed, Sammy, who hadn't undressed, went to the closet and came back holding strands of rope with loops at the ends.

They had stopped turning off the lights long ago. Occasionally he even left the shade up. The streets around the docks were deserted at night.

Seeing the rope, Ada sat up, folding her arms over her heavy breasts.

Samuel Robinwood stopped in his tracks and stared at her until she relaxed and lay back down. It was only Sammy, and he still had his tie on. He came up and, nimble as a surgeon suturing an appendix, he secured Ada's wrists and ankles to the brass posts while she held herself still.

Once more he turned. This time what he held up before her eyes was his thin black belt, though he looked comic dressed as he still was in his black pants and white shirt, with its pinned sleeve, his upper lip sweaty.

No, Ada said.

But he understood what she really meant.

~

She refused to see him again.

She bathed in salts. She douched. She stayed celibate for a month. For a month she went to mass every morning, and prayed late into the evening for Jesus' return.

But when, after several weeks, the need for company reasserted itself, Ada began picking up men at the restaurant and bringing them home until Mr. Elba finally fired her. She didn't care; she'd had enough of that. She took a job at a diner, where she worked mornings, leaving her nights free.

Eventually the community found out. People saw her on the street in the company of strangers. Her clothes had been outrageous enough. The gears of gossip began grinding, and nothing could stand up to them. Women snubbed her. Mrs. Prokop in the store, and people at church whom she hardly knew, glared.

At church, she weathered the parishioners' frowns because she understood: their lives were hard, yet they obeyed while she had strayed. She would never again find a comfortable haven among them, but did that matter? She wasn't there to worship them. Every Sunday she knelt under the roar of airplanes drowning out the choir and said her rosary, one prayer for each bead: for Alex, for Paul, for Anton, for me.

Exiled from home and from God, who was a Man and forgave men their sins long before He'd pardon a woman, she prayed to Mary who knew what it was to be frightened and alone in a foreign country.

What was there about desire that it should be punished? She loved losing herself, even in Sammy's one arm. Those minutes of erasure were evensong and compline in Latin by candlelight. Why should the Lord begrudge her when the rest of her time was eaten up by work and responsibilities? When the dead are raised incorruptible from their graves, first thing they'll do is pair off and drop to the ground for a fuck.

Yet, for all her rationalizations, peace eluded her, and in time Adriana climbed down from her senses. She quit men entirely—but for a single lapse, which bound me to the Kruks more tightly than ever.

And once the men really were gone, Jesus returned. Ada never could decide if she'd made a fair swap.

Alex and I held many of our best conversations walking along the railroad tracks a few blocks from his house. Every few minutes a train roared by and we'd stop and stare and imagine ourselves swept up in its wake, carried down the Eastern corridor to Philadelphia, Washington, Newport News, Charleston, and down to Florida, to the Keys. Every name heralded a different universe of fantasies: from the Liberty Bell in Philly to the monuments of D.C. to who knows what in Newport News, to the fabulous Keys! Some genius dreamed that name, inciting the lust of ten million boys whose culminating adventures played out in Key Largo, with rifles and women in a house by the sea in a storm; and even we, veterans of such singular games as Secret Police, indulged in the common fare of boyish speculation, imagining ourselves other, larger, huge with power, knowing the secrets Ada so painfully bought from her men. For a few minutes we stopped being scared, stopped running hunched down the valley of shadows, whipped by impulses and terrified by the unknown forces controlling the lives of the people around us. For as long as the echo of that train dinned down our day, for just that long, we were changed, made better, suddenly equals to any, in knowledge, power, and dreams.

Then it was gone and we were left to talk about the world as we really found it. Alex told ironic stories about the mother he met for breakfast in the morning and the woman he sometimes listened to across the hall at night. He seemed almost boastful about the business, as though he were lucky to have so much of the mystery of adulthood dissipated early, and I found myself increasingly interested in the images he conjured of Ada. I saw her panting, disheveled, half-drunk and half-naked, her white shirt unbuttoned to her waist, looking up at me from under the curtain of hair.

My father, meanwhile, had recently begun talking about moving us to Fort Hills, and as I told Alex about this, I said that of course I intended to return to the neighborhood every weekend.

It was a late afternoon in mid-November, around Thanksgiving, and the tracks were quilted with greenish yellow and brown leaves the sun licked with fire.

But Alex didn't hear me. He was caught up in trying to figure out all that his mother brought before him, and he kept returning to it, increasingly, with a note of anger creeping in through the cracks.

"God thing worries me, " he said, lighting a cig with a gloved hand.

"Pictures of Jesus?"

"You don't know. It's huge. Postcards are only a part of it. She looks at me and half the time I don't know what she's seeing but it isn't me."

"OWS," I said.

He shrugged. "Sure, OWS, definitely. But getting worse."

OWS stood for Old World Syndrome, our code for those adult behaviors we could explain no other way—words like trauma and manic depression being unfamiliar to us.

"It's the fucking past," he said, stopping behind the A & P lot.

"What kind of car you want?" he asked, looking out at our options.

"Buick," I said without a second thought.

"Serious? No way. More than a 'vette?"

I regarded the platoon of Fords and Chryslers below.

"Yeah."

"Been thinking of California," Alex said.

"Running away?"

"No. Business," he snapped.

I nodded. California sounded nearly as fabulous as the Keys.

"What about the Keys?"

"Too many hurricanes."

There'd been a tropical storm in the news the previous week that had hit the Florida coast.

"Earthquakes, amico."

"Not as bad."

In the distance a whistle sounded and we both stared down the track at the bright white light rushing toward us.

6

When she heard that Anton was finally coming to town Ada must have felt an echo of longing. The poet who'd taken her to the opera to hear *La Boheme*, with whom she'd flirted in the displaced persons camp, who'd gone to England where he had become, so she heard, a professor of literature, was scheduled to perform at the National Home the second weekend in March: Sunday at four in the afternoon.

Unlike our peers, we had no free time on weekends: between Saturday school, scouts, church, religious instruction, and public events, we lived inside an ethnic storm system where the weather was always turbulent.

There was an air of excitement surrounding Anton's appearance. He was coming from England, where he had published some poems and stories in English, as well as articles on the peculiar triumvirate of Charles Dickens, T. S. Eliot, and Isaiah Berlin—the names stood out unmistakably among the usual roster of *itches* and *atskys* and *isms*. There were rumors he'd spent time at Cambridge and Oxford. Recognizable pedigrees were rare enough anywhere in Roosevelt: that one of "our own," as even my father referred to him, had received the faintest recognition from the outside world was the subject of headlines. The community felt particularly invisible at the time and it was convinced the American media had it in for them. Had Anton been a Nobel Prize winner, he couldn't have received a bigger build-up.

Nothing he might say could have satisfied the huge hunger his audience brought into the small auditorium above the basement tavern that afternoon. After picking up Ada and Alex, we arrived early to get good seats, but so many had been even more eager that we wound up in the last row.

No lights were dimmed in the hall of three hundred heavy-breathing Slavs as the blue curtain was drawn to reveal a trembling Mr. Kowal, whose job it was to introduce the guest of honor. As if enough had not already been said by the priest and in the papers, Mr. Kowal proceeded to rehearse in detail the poet's life and devotions to the community. He compared his three or four English-language publications to the vast oeuvre of Joseph Conrad. The names of Maeterlink and Ibsen were invoked. As the legion of superlatives crescendoed, the crowd, incapable of containing itself, erupted in whistles and applause, drowning out the bewildered speaker, who finally shrugged his shoulders and, with a slight bow and flourish, yielded the floor to our honored guest.

It took only a few seconds to realize how high we would all be left to dry; and to be fair, no one, not President Kennedy or Dwight D. Eisenhower or even J. Edgar Hoover, to name three heroes among the émigrés, could have lived up to the expectations of that crowd. That the diminutive, almost-elfin gentleman in the green blazer who stepped out of the wings to face the mob was sweating was clear even to me in the back row. His first move was to wipe his face with a handkerchief, which gave us enough time to quiet down. A hush as loud as the earlier roar claimed the hall. Some of the more literary ladies had taken out pens and notebooks in order to record the prophet's precious pronouncements.

"Ladies and gentlemen." The first words were themselves a shock. English. He was speaking in English. And for the next thirty-five minutes Anton talked, in precise if stylized English, about the importance of cultivating an appreciation for the literary heritage of one's new homeland. His voice was soft; not even the microphone could multiply the decibels sufficiently to give his talk some mechanical oomph in compensation for the absence of rhetorical firepower. Instead of the rousing patriotic screed for which the émigrés had hoped, which they so desparately needed, living as they did in an enveloping silence, inside a culture that acted as though they weren't there, they listened, with mounting and audible impatience, to a thoughtful and slightly suggestive lecture on Walt Whitman and the limits of prosodic freedom. No one even noticed this remarkable feat was conducted without reference to a single sheet of paper or note card: Anton had memorized his talk. At the end, when he invited questions from the audience, after a long pause, a hand went up:

"What do you think of the political prospects for us in the foreseeable future?"

Anton seemed to twitch uncomfortably. He thrust his hands into the pockets of his green jacket and leaned back on the balls of his feet. For the first time it looked like he was speaking to the audience from on high.

"Alas, I am not Nostrodamus. I have come here," he said in a voice that suddenly sounded as familiar as my mother's singing, "to tell you about worlds beyond politics. I know we have duties to the past. To know history is essential: without that, there can be no conscience. And without conscience, there can be no self. But I invite you to notice there are other ways of being, different ways of viewing experience. I know you're afraid of losing yourselves inside the new language. Using it may feel like a case of the disappearing sickness. But it is not the same thing at all. It can even be an intensification of who you are ..."

He stopped. It was as though someone signaled him that he'd bombed, that the audience had switched him off long ago.

"Thank you. You've been very kind. If any of you wish to discuss this further, I'll be downstairs in a minute."

The disappointed crowd applauded the false Messiah lethargically and before the curtain had closed on his slight figure, people began putting on their jackets and rushing to the door. No one wanted to be on that floor when he came out. Not even Ada. I don't know if it was her disappointment in Anton's talk, or guilt about her involvement with Sammy, but the rest of us could barely keep up with her as she rushed for the car.

On the ride home, instead of the usual heated debate, silence held us in her boney arms. Finally Ada hissed:

"He sold himself to the English."

After a moment, Father said:

"I thought he spoke well. But I couldn't understand everything. His accent," he said sympathetically, as though the burden of a British accent were yet another slight to be born by the heroic émigrés. Ada looked glum and said nothing more. When we dropped the Kruks off, she barely nodded farewell.

"See ya," said Alex.

Early the next morning, after her sons had left, Ada answered the doorbell and found Anton standing there. He was wearing his green blazer, holding a bouquet of snapdragons in one hand and a battered leather briefcase in the other.

Her hand rose to her mouth and she stepped back.

"May I come in?"

"Of course, come in," she said, leading him through the kitchen to the living room, whose paint had began peeling.

Anton seemed not to notice the shabby surroundings. His eyes never left Ada, whose turn it now was to twitch.

"Yes, well," he said. "This could be awkward, so let's not. I know what you and everybody here thought of my lecture. Doesn't matter. I said what I did, and that's done. And I've heard about Lev. I'm sorry. Thought much better of him, frankly. War changes people, and emigration does too.

"Changed me, you see. Sold myself to the Brits. That's what people say. Not a bad group to pawn yourself to, so long as you don't lose the ticket. Lovely things in their culture. Lovely. And since they know practically nothing about ours, I sometimes find myself distinctly at an advantage."

They were sitting on the sofa now.

He looked around at the walls.

"Well, who's the painter?"

"My son Alex."

"Not bad, Ada. Never know who anyone will become until they become it."

His features were small and fine and she could tell he was laboring hard to make her feel comfortable, as though it were his apartment. How gray his temples were! The last time she'd seen him he was a flaming boy full of fantasies about literature.

Why was she afraid of him?

As if reading her mind, he said:

"Don't be afraid. I promise I won't tell you anything more about Walt Whitman, or even Emily Dickinson, not this morning."

She forced herself to shake her head. What was this paralysis?

"Ada, I have a crazy thing to say. Believe me, it's a crazy thing. You don't have to answer. Take all the time, all the time. I'm going to New York for a few days, visiting old friends, talks at the societies, where they won't run away from me."

Ada, still in her red woolen housecoat and red slippers, had not even put on her make-up. Finally she recovered her voice:

"What could it possibly be, Anton?"

"That voice hasn't changed. Many ways less changed than you think. We haven't been able to go home, that's true. But life hasn't been entirely horrible since the war. I have a decent job at a vocational college. City's ugly, students aren't Einsteins, but summers I hike in the Lake district and visit the Reading Room at the British Museum.

"To the point, Ada," he said, nervous, plucking at his tie. "I'd like you to come back to England with me. I've waited a long time to ask you because ... well, because of a lot things, but now everything's ready and I'm relatively secure, and I think you would like it."

Ada ricocheted back: this wasn't what she'd expected.

After another long silence, she said:

"Poets get an idea, a few words. It's not like that."

Anton kept his eyes fixed on the carpet. Then he tugged at his trousers and put his hands on his knees and leaned forward.

"Of course. But here's what I ask. I'm going to leave you something."

He picked up his briefcase, unlatched it, and took out what looked like a paperback.

"Magazine. Story I wrote. I want you to read it. Then let me stop next week."

She shook her head.

"Something you wrote in a magazine?"

"I know how it is to live in a billboard. Flat. Nobody sees you around. You're right. Arrogant. Read it anyway."

He stood up.

Ada walked him to the door.

"Good-bye," he said warmly, offering his hand. "It has been very nice. I look forward."

Ada shook her head. Then she leaned close and kissed him on the cheek.

After he'd gone, she glanced at the kitchen clock. She had to get ready for work. She worked nearly all the time now, two shifts, leaving at ten and not returning until late.

That day business was slow. In March people's appetite for dining out was at its nadir. Several times during the day her thoughts drifted to Anton and she shook her head. So the world; things just kept happening.

She got home around ten to find both her sons in front of the television, which she immediately turned off. Ignoring their complaints, she sent them to their room, washed, and prepared for bed. She could hear Viktor moving about behind his closed door.

Finally, in bed, she remembered the magazine Anton had left her and she got up and padded into the living room. Back under the blankets, she looked at the cover: an abstract painting showing an image of Dante's head exploding into a thousand fragments. She knew the head was Dante's because of a caption on the inside.

She found Anton's name in the table of contents and next to it the title: "The Ambassador of the Dead." She lingered over this for a few minutes before turning to the page, deep in the middle of the thickish journal.

There was the title. She read the first line and gasped. She sat up. That was her name in the first sentence. Adriana. Her name. And not just her name. She knew the place he was describing, and the people! They were her family. Her heart raced as though she had just jumped from a plane; and in order for the chute to open, she read on.

The Ambassador of the Dead

1

Adriana was born in the city of Resurrection on the river Memory, the eldest of nine children. A tall girl with a long neck, spidery fingers, and skinny legs, her nickname was giraffe, which she bore as gracefully as she did most things. Her father, Dr. Taras Sich, himself the son of freed serfs who'd worked his way out of the village to become a judge, and her mother, Dr. Irina Buk, a teacher and cultural booster from a similar background, had given their daughter a confidence about her place in the world that she never lost, though she often felt the world a reluctant partner in the bargain. However, she forgave the world its failings since she herself had from an early age moved beyond it, establishing a link to the larger and infinitely more powerful shadow empire of the dead.

In one of the last normal seasons of Ada's life, a year before the Famine, her family summered at a house on the Black Sea. Framed by prodigal oaks and bleached by endless light, the gabled building stood with windows open, breathing in the salt breeze blowing off the water beyond the dunes. At dawn, while everyone still slept, seven-year-old Adriana slipped out of the house. Followed by Pan Micho, the beekeeper's cat, who loved carrots, the girl loped down the path to the beach. She passed anthills big as her rocking horse and paused to watch hummingbirds spearing bee balm, its petals dry tears of blood.

Standing on a dune, staring out at the water, she yanked the wing of the red kerchief she'd tied minutes earlier. It slipped off, spilling waves of gold hair. She wanted the damp air everywhere. She watched the bright, foaming manes of the horses—a tumult of plumes and sabers—and the mirage of bundled horizons set her heart pounding louder than the surf as she imagined herself carried across on a raft twined of starfish and driftwood. The aphrodisiac wind unspooled skeins of lust for a future in which her gifts would enroll her in the log of the blessed.

A naked woman with brackish red hair rose from the sand a few feet away and hastened to the water, startling Ada. She stared: where had she seen her before? Maybe back in the city.

A gull landed nearby. It cocked one orange eye in her direction, then turned its neck as though to confirm the sight with the other, which blinked in angry recognition. Had they met before? The bird's hooked beak opened and shut soundlessly. It swiveled its neck several more times, leaned on one foot, then the other until, disgusted, it pushed off into the air. What might it be like to follow it? She'd ask her friend Slava, the one person she knew who'd actually flown.

Slava, Queen of the Winds, as she liked to be called, was Ada's age. She and her family stayed at the hotel. Last year, alone on the beach, she'd been caught by a sudden tornado. Sucked into a funneling cloud that whirled her like an egg beater, she'd been set down on a nest of woven straw, with an eagle feather in her fist. The others were in the house when the twister appeared. Hearing the fury of the storm, and noticing the girl was missing, they ran out only to find the child ruffled but smiling, a hundred yards from where they'd last seen her. Slava later told Ada she'd watched her dead grandfather riding a horse down a porch of floating debris: she claimed he swooped her up in his arms and kissed her without dropping his sword. She pointed to the crimson crescent on her cheek where his mustaches had scraped her.

Ada dropped to the sand to await her friend. She wrapped her thin arms around her knees and balanced her chin between them. She tried curling her tongue but it stayed flat as a sand dollar. A beetle crawled toward her, its jaws opening and shutting like hedge clippers. Ada plucked a stalk and thrust it at the bug until it clamped on. She hoisted it up slowly.

At that moment Pan Micho leaped out of the grass and swatted the beetle to the sand.

"Ada!" Her friend Slava was on her way.

The naked woman rose from the whitecaps and Ada stared at the water drizzling from the sponge between her legs.

"Who's that?" Slava asked.

"Don't you know?"

The woman strutted past the gawking girls.

Slava was even skinnier than Adriana. She lived on the other side of the country, in the middle of the heartland that had given Ukraine its reputation as Europe's food pantry, where wheat stalks shivered in the wind like slivers of a shattered sun, the gold stained red from centuries of slaughter.

Slava's father, a doctor, was a spare man with a monocle and a perpetual sniffle. When he came for tarok, he always brought new picture books. He had so many, Ada imagined he lived in a library. The girls pored over them while the adults played cards. Sometimes Slava's father would have a sneezing fit and the game would be interrupted until the humor spent itself.

The nude dressed, grabbed her towel, and walked off, and the girls turned to more important matters. Together they gathered crabs filleted by gulls while the tide receded like a creature slipping from the edge of the world, fingers losing grip of the dunes. They then sat down to the business of building cities. By lunch time, however, dynasties of sand castles lay scattered like medieval kingdoms stormed by giants. The girls plunged into the sea to wash themselves. Floating on their backs, they watched the shore dissolve under the water's tongue, and jellyfish nuzzled against them.

At the house Adriana's mother urged Slava to eat her lunch. Slava replied with a giggle and a shake of the head.

"Careful. You'll catch the disappearing sickness," said Dr. Buk. To which Slava smiled and, slipping her arm around Ada, carried her off back to the sea. She must have been part nymph because every chance she got she headed for water. Evenings, Adriana's mother boiled water and filled the zinc tub while both girls sat on the floor, chatting with porcelain dolls. The first time Slava stripped off her dress, Adriana noticed a birthmark on her belly shaped unmistakably like a sea horse.

"That's Horace," Slava said.

Lying in bed, Adriana felt the sea lifting her like her father's arms. The day's images roamed under her lids. Falling asleep, she kept seeing the naked woman diving into the water, hair hissing as she hit the waves.

The next day Ada again raced to the sea. This time it was covered with blue and white shells, scalloped and smooth, round and oblong, heavy as marble and fragile as feathers. In the middle, small as a prayer book, lay a black Leica she imagined some tourist dropping when the yacht pitched just as he was snapping a dolphin. She hurried forward, but before she could reach it, a wave snatched the camera, and most of the shells, away.

"Ada!"

Mother calling.

She walked resentfully back to the house, entering through the french doors.

Both her parents were rushing about the living room when she came in.

"Oh, dear, you forgot," her mother said, giving her a look, then turning away to rearrange a blue glass vasc stuffed with birds of paradise on the burlwood grand.

Various brothers and sisters sprawled and crawled around the floor, creating confusion.

Her father, who was conferring with the gardener, waved. She studied his long, elegant form. He was dressed in gray, with rhinoceros leather shoes, a shiny silver vest, and a darker squirrel-colored jacket and trousers.

A stranger who'd been hanging back in the shadows came forward. He wore a white shirt with french cuffs and a ruffled front.

His shaggy hair was dirty while his boots looked like they had at most one walk left before expiring. He clicked his heels pretentiously, bowed low enough to lick the tiles, and proffered a handful of limp fingers.

"Who are you?" she asked.

His thick lips curled down. She'd insulted him.

"I am the painter."

"The portrait, Ada, the portrait," her mother chirped.

"Yes, come stand here, child," said Dr. Sich.

Grief-stricken, Ada did as she was told. No sea today. Dullest business. Standing for two hours while this boob drew and dabbed, chattering, with nothing to say.

"Riots in Vienna," the man offered.

Ada shuddered. Riots in Vienna. Just the news she wanted to hear. Riots in Vienna! Vacation, she was on vacation. As in: to vacate the old life. As in: to forget the world.

"Doesn't surprise me," her father replied curtly. It seemed he too wanted to keep the world at bay a while. What relief. Better silence than the strain of empty patter.

"Gather up," her mother clapped her hands.

The family formed a united front. Even young Orest kept it zipped until, unable to contain himself, he cried in a falsetto:

"Mother, why do you think my eyes are turning yellow and what should I do about it?"

They stood there breathing in perfume and laundry soap, hearing the sea and the birds, watching butterflies draining the bee balm through open doors behind the angry artist lashing the canvas.

After a while the painter, who'd aged a decade since starting this project, waved them over to see what his hand had wrought. He'd entered the spirit of the game, and as the family marveled at the result, he leaned back against the piano arms akimbo, silent.

Ada brooded over how much larger than herself loomed her mother and father, how much more handsome and finished they appeared. She frowned at her own face with unfeigned contempt: the blond hair, the almond-shaped green eyes set so wide apart it made her high cheeks look like the twin poles of a boomerang. And the chin: so square you could rest a tea cup on it. Oh and the legs and neck of a giraffe, definitely. These were the gifts God had given her and she knew she should be thankful. Luckily, she was pleased with herself no matter how the world saw her. Turning her back on the painter, whose smugness she found insulting, she asked her mother:

"May I go to the beach now?"

"What, oh, yes, isn't this a little wonderful, dear?" she said to her husband, and the two of them looked to the painter, whose thoughts had grown homicidal. Sweeping his hair off his forehead, he forced a smile. One morning, one portrait—that was his motto. He had chosen it. If this led him to the summer homes of philistines, so be it, he had wanted this life.

The satisfied couple, meanwhile, hoisted their hands over their heads and applauded.

On this same trip to the coast, which once belonged to the tsars and tsarinas of legend—extraordinary beings who flaunted their affection for each other with gifts of mountains and villages—Dr. Sich, a lapsed mystic and former seminarian, took Ada on a visit to a monastery. Most were closed to women but her father was an important man, and even the monks of Crimea had heard of him. When he arrived, in his summer caftan and flowing white pants, holding his daughter's hand, they opened both doors. The monk who showed them around claimed to count his age in centuries, which Dr. Sich certainly didn't believe, though he kept his skepticism in check, as he did nearly every thought that might be counted negative.

Decades later, Ada still remembered an icon of the Annunciation: a haggard Gabriel addresses an anxious Mary sitting on a gold throne, somber and fingering the red fabric of the temple veil symbolizing the mortal flesh she was destined to wrap around her son's immortal spirit. The halos circumnavigating the heads of the beatified gleamed, and the laser of light cutting into her belly passed through a dove and shaped a shield around the uncreated form blooming inside her. She felt her own conception had been like that—some force had secretly penetrated her mother's scarred belly, turning her into one of the pure, shining, elect.

Unlike most Catholic girls, however, who pass through a period when they imagine themselves becoming nuns, Ada found herself unaccountably drawn to images of the beautiful Magdalene.

Important people began visiting her father. She knew they were important because she was not invited to tea. She watched the parade of bulbous men in white linen, their grave mouths pouting like the long spout of the watering can the gardener used on the phalaeonopsis. They discussed politics; she knew that. She heard the names of Vynko, Petla, and Stalin whose picture was on every wall of her school. Names for the history books, maybe, but not fit for living rooms. No, this did not make her happy.

Excluded from the circle of adult concerns, Ada turned to books. That summer she graduated from Pippi Longstocking to Selma Lagerlöf. As the sun waned, she sprawled across the wicker chaise on the verandah swallowed up inside *The Saga of Gösta Borling.*

Too soon the time came for them to return to the city. Riding to the train station in the horse-drawn wagon, sitting alongside her mother, across from the brood of burbling sibs, Ada listened to wheels reading the road's braille and watched as long-legged cranes raced across a field of dried grass. The afternoon's only breeze was her mother's breath on her neck. Biting her cheese sandwich, she gazed around triumphantly. This was her country: no matter where she traveled within it, she was home.

The wagon was drawn by two drab drays. The driver, whose bobbing head registered ruts in the road, had long gray hair and a steel wool beard hanging to his waist. Gypsy from Old Town. So she thought. He spat and laughed at nothing at all. The judge, who sat beside him, pulled out some chewing tobacco, and the men celebrated its bitterness.

Dr. Sich asked him where he was from.

"Oh, you won't know it," the man waved his hand.

Ada tore off a hunk of bread and tossed it into the stream.

"No?"

"No, I come from the east. My father was a king."

The judge chuckled.

The driver spat:

"By now I suppose I must be the king—surely my father is dead. And who are you?" he asked Ada.

"That's just the giraffe," said Dr. Sich.

"Listen, giraffe, you know they say this is where Saint Andrew came after your Lord and Savior went to Heaven."

"Who was Saint Andrew?"

"Oh, it's true, then?"

"What?"

"The waters of the world are evaporating. Soon all the oceans will be dry."

"Why do you say that?" asked Dr. Sich.

"Because people are forgetting. My job, I see people, nobody remembers anymore."

"What does that have to do with the oceans?"

"Everything that has ever happened is written in water. Water is the world's memory. Have you ever found yourself thinking about something you'd never seen?"

Dr. Sich nodded.

"Well, it's because some water slipped into your ear. But when people start to forget, it means the water level is going down."

"Once more. Who is Saint Andrew?" Ada insisted.

"First apostle of your savior, Jesus Christ."

"Why do you say my savior? And why is everyone trying to give me religion?" the girl asked.

"I pray to Allah," the old man replied thoughtfully.

"Did you and your father fight?" Dr. Sich asked.

"Never. I wanted to travel, see God's earth."

"How do you live?"

"Everywhere I go I meet people who knew my father," he said

simply. "They lend a hand. If I need it. Which I rarely do. It's the family. Genghis Khan, you see."

"Ah, the Khan family."

"So they say. Me, I don't make much of that kind of thing."

"Is there anything I can do for you?"

The old man turned and looked at Ada's father with a wet eye.

"You'd be surprised how much an old cab man knows. See that house over there?" He pointed his whip at a ragged building of black stone on a hill above the road. Beyond it, the sun shimmered a final orange before sinking out of sight.

"Belongs to my cousin. My father raised him. Father was loved and love has great power."

Ada felt the lungs of the clouds draw a breath. It was one of those moments in which you feel yourself inside your own life as though you were on stage, upheld by a hundred pairs of eyes.

The driver turned to Ada and said, "Remember, giraffe: in the world there are people who can help you when you're in trouble, but you have to know where to find them, and you must know how to speak your mind.

"There's a story about that house," he went on, "Do you want to hear it?"

Ada nodded.

At the train station, her father tipped him generously.

Sitting at the other end of the platform, Ada noticed the woman with the brackish red hair.

2

She never saw the Black Sea again. Over the next years, her father grew increasingly absorbed in his work.

She knew that something was wrong when the following summer, instead of being dispatched to her mother's father's farm in Laski, they stayed home in the city. "There's no food in the countryside," her mother explained. That year they too subsisted on rations, though the children didn't pay much attention to such things. But Ada noticed how serious both her parents looked, and she heard them speaking among themselves of funerals and famine. The troubles seemed distant, and on their way.

And yet, life in the city before the war also included many delicious routines. Voskresene on the River Pamiat was a thousand years old and it knew how to entertain its residents: summer's end was prelude to the banquets of autumn. She missed Slava but soon there were piano lessons, as well as ballet, where her giraffe's legs became assets. A spell in the park after school where Ada gathered chestnuts for the cook to roast was followed by a round of tag with her brothers and sisters at home. Viktor was good at inventing games: he was the one who dreamed up Secret Police, which they added to a repertoire of more traditional sports, such as bobbing for apples and pin the tail on the commissar.

As the eldest child, Ada enjoyed special privileges. She was the first to move from the children's table in the kitchen to sit with the grown-ups in the dining room where dinner was a rather formal affair and the silver was used nightly. She complained to her brothers and sisters about having to sit up straight and carry the spoon to her lips instead of hunching down to slurp it. "You wouldn't like it," she assured the others diplomatically.

Moreover, you had to listen to endless political blather. There were guests nearly every night, including generals and bishops, writers and ministers, and conversations switched easily from Ukrainian to Polish, French to Russian. The people around her father's table were trying to build a country, and the business sounded far harder than sand castles. She learned one history at home, another in school.

"Malov's dead. Watch out, " a woman said at dinner one evening, and the next day her father was arrested, though he was released in just a few days.

Over the years, dinner seemed a roll call of disappeared or assassinated politicians:

"The minister's gone. Khruschev's there now. He says the party's spotless. The empire's back."

"But that's the capital's problem. We deal with the others."

Dinner conversations were often breathless and emotional. While the maid carried out platters of roast beef and "fingers"—strips of boiled dough—the guests spoke about things they'd seen, and what they'd seen was rarely pretty. Ada observed more than one grown man weeping softly while repeating a litany of names of people who'd either been executed or disappeared.

Her father worked with the NDO—the National Democratic Organization—and because of this he was occasionally arrested, though he'd never spent more than a week in jail. Nevertheless, he sometimes turned to her and said loudly:

"The names don't matter, dear. The only thing that counts is kindness."

While dining with adults was generally a burden, an extension of school, what Ada loved was the room itself. High-ceilinged, its pale blue walls were hung with paintings by Vasily Sternberg, a friend of the poet Shevchenko, and Kapiton Pavlov who'd been a teacher of Gogol's. One of the paintings showed a blind musician seated in a dark room playing a stringed instrument and singing while a family of peasants, their faces long and thin, huddled around as though they were the fuel his songs consumed.

The poet Anton took her to concerts at the Opera House, where she heard *La Boheme*. He was several years older than Adriana and had been a friend of the family for as long as she could remember. He wasn't handsome, but he had style: he came at the world severely, rejecting those daily matters, from housekeeping to the war itself, as traps for his spirit laid by demons of a low order, and so beneath his notice. His clothes never fit: the jackets were always too small and the pants too large. Once she asked him why this was and he explained that he got the coat from his younger brother and the trousers from his older one. Sometimes he reversed the equation. But, he assured her, though he wasn't the best dressed man in town, he had other gifts. He read many languages, including English, and he loved Hart Crane and Whitman. He would recite to her in English while they walked down the wide street to the Opera House. In his mouth, the language was a clash of crazy sounds.

One day he appeared at the door more disheveled than ever. His coat had black schmutz all over the front, and his shoes were covered in mud. He held something close to his chest and his eyes sprayed light. His first book had just appeared. He thrust a copy at her.

"*Polycronicon*," Ada read from the cover. "What's that?"

"Never mind. One day you will be able to read my poems in English. I promise you."

"No I won't," she flirted.

"Why not?" the crestfallen poet asked.

"I don't like modern poetry."

Yet she remained a reader, inhaling poems and novels in translations. She loved Pearl Buck and John Steinbeck.

Anton lived in the Jewish quarter and lately he'd begun studying the Kabbala. He raved to Ada about a book called the *Zohar*, prattling about *ein sof* and the *ten sephiroth*, about *keter, hokhmah, binah, gevurah,* and *tifferet*: bolts of weird language flew from his lips.

He told her wild stories about conversations with God and he said he knew why so many around them were suffering: "It goes back to the seventeenth century, to the uprising. They killed thousands of innocents. Women. Children. Jews. Catholics. These things have their effect. You think God forgets? Until we face our own sins we'll never find peace."

Ada stared at his face, bright with fanatical light. He was her savior—she sensed it. But whenever she leaned too close, he pulled away, as though frightened of her body.

Her body: no myth foretells a girl her body's changes. Ada spent hours studying her naked form using her mother's silver hand mirror, as though she could learn to calculate how men would react if her breasts were to swell another few centimeters. So far, each millimeter was money in the bank. While there were days she wished no eyes widened when she passed, mainly she enjoyed the slow outward spread of her magnetic field. For a time her own image mesmerized her and she found it impossible to concentrate in the vicinity of a mirror.

If only her father didn't work so much. He came home long after the sun had set over their small city, trapped on the razor's edge between Europe and Russia. "We're Europeans," he often said at dinner, to which everyone nodded without necessarily understanding his vehemence. "Paris, now that's a city," he said to Ada. From him she learned about Vienna and London, Rome and Jerusalem, New Delhi and New York. The world's great cities formed a kind of club in her mind and she imagined herself moving constantly, visiting Buckingham Palace one morning, St. Peter's the next. She loved it when he was home for dinner, and most days she waited for him at the window until he returned. She'd throw herself at him and sponge him with kisses.

"I see the opera is having an effect on you," he said, not really disapproving. He explained that for adults life was one endless school day.

"But how can you do your homework if you're never home?" the girl countered.

As it turned out, the next lesson was violence. It arrived overnight—though she'd seen the trouble gathering for years. There was shooting in the streets, and planes roared down like monstrous birds laying bombs. One day, her brother Viktor, who studied at the gymnasium, didn't come home. Her mother, who taught in the grade school, canvassed the city for word of his whereabouts. Both soldiers and partisans used kidnapping as a recruitment tactic. Unable to find him, she had no choice but to return to work, though she herself hadn't been feeling well lately.

Sometimes the children found themselves alone in the apartment during an air raid. Ada sat in the closet with her brothers and sisters, singing to drown out the explosions. Some Silly Lisle song about a bucket with a hole in it. Bombs whistled outside. Orest had two thumbs in his mouth. Halia was talking to her father's hat. And Ada stared at a huge Advent card showing a gigantic chateau with twenty-five windows overlooking a pond on which families skated happily. Across the street, the church tower exploded, sending stones through their window. From where does the harshness of the world arise? What is the root cause of our suffering? She fought back tears by being bad: she opened all the windows, beginning with December 1st. But the planes didn't leave. What would it take? Didn't they know it was just her? Why are they attacking *me*? Ada wondered. What happened to the people who sent the planes? Anything? She wiped her nose with the back of her hand. When would her mother be home? All the forces of the world arrayed against her, so she licked the nub of a green pop.

There were answers to nearly all of her questions. Anton once explained that the matter had to be considered on several planes—the historical, the moral, and the spiritual. Historical questions dealt with matters of power, with the theft of resources and enslavement of populations. The moral plane focused on the consequences of an individual's actions; on what one did to others, how one treated them. The spiritual sphere, meanwhile, concerned one's relationship with God. There are no accidents, he insisted. Every hair is numbered!

His confidence did nothing to calm Ada's fears.

3

Soon after the war started, Dr. Irina Buk sent her children out of the city to stay with various relatives in the countryside. Ada's mother believed she was moving them away from the front. By then, however, the front was gone and the war was everywhere.

Ada went to live with her aunt, a knotty woman with a face shriveled and cratered as the inside of a walnut. Her mother's sister lived in a two-room house with no electricity and a thatched roof near the edge of a village consisting of two dozen cottages surrounded by a sprawl of farms. The windows in the building were small and the door didn't close properly. On cold nights the goats and chickens slept indoors, upsetting the dogs who chased the birds around until her aunt finally dragged the mutts into the bed that the two women shared. "Plenty room," she assured Ada, who frequently woke with her arms wrapped around Brovko's black neck.

Her aunt had no children and envied Ada's mother the size of her brood. That's how it was—people in the city had more of everything while good country folk went begging. No wonder there had been a revolution. Yet she was glad for Ada's company, and when she discovered the girl was literate she dragged out the bible her husband had left her and made Ada read from it while she prepared their dinner of corn meal and meats. She loved the story of Noah. "You are the sons of Noah," she told the dogs and chickens, crossing herself, then making the sign of the cross over the animals. The rooster, aggressively pagan, cocoricooed in protest.

Far from being a haven, the village swarmed with military. Soldiers rutted the snow-driven streets while gun-toting men without uniforms haunted the square. Her aunt ignored them.

"It's men's business," she said, waving them away with her hand. "They're all headed to hell anyway."

They walked through the village, carrying eggs to the churner who bartered for butter. Chickens scrambled at their feet, squabbling like kids. As they passed the largest house in the street, Ada noticed soldiers gathered around its massive brown door, smoking and laughing and stamping their boots in snow peppered with butts and discarded bottles.

"Never go near there," her aunt said. "That's where they keep their women."

Her aunt kept her busy with sewing, mending rugs and shirts, and making candles from phosphor-colored beeswax. While her niece worked, the old woman sat beside her pouring forth a litany of complaints about her brothers and sisters. "My brother, he's got all the money," she told Ada. "But he's a selfish bastard who never cared about another soul in his entire life. He'd never understand why I'm helping you."

Ada was about to protest that he'd taken in two of her brothers but thought better of it.

She loved skating at night. One evening, after scraping the supper plates and scattering meal on the ice for the chickens, she grabbed the wooden skates hanging near the fireplace, along with the broom, and set off for the pond.

She sat on the frozen snow and put on her skates. Drifts covered the ice and she realized she should have brought along a shovel. She picked up the broom and pushed it before her until she'd cleared a path. The cold left her giddy and short of breath. She looked up at the stars, which covered the night sky like scattered flakes. How close everybody seemed—she could feel them all, her mother and father and every one of her siblings—as though they weren't far at all, as if distance didn't matter, because they lived inside her. She warmed quickly. She could feel her cheeks redden, as though heat were a color. Alone on the ice under the moon she again felt herself blessed, a daughter of the elements, and the war someone else's problem. Soon she'd cleared an elaborate course for herself across which she glided with rough grace, lost in the stylized motion. She hummed a song about campfires, remembering summers playing on the beach along the Black Sea in the Crimea with her friend Slava. Funny to think of sand while surrounded by snow. She shut her eyes and remembered the monastery, and the beekeeper's cat, and the naked redhead diving into the waves. Suddenly she began sneezing. Time to go. She swung toward the bank where she sat down, peeled off her skates, struggled back into her boots, and set out for home.

The night shone like a church at Christmas and she watched wind skimming stray leaves across the snow.

A loud jeep idled in the field. Strange. What was it doing there, in the middle of nothing? She'd ridden in a car only once: an uncle's black Bentley had been the first in the region and when he took the children for a ride, she'd felt proud waving to the peasants who pressed around the windows. Now she shuffled forward, boots crunching the ground. As she bent to peer into the window, the door opened and she was thrown back. The broom flew out of her hands as she sank into the snow. Then he was on her, a wolf in uniform. Light flashed off his buttons and medals. His beard scratched her cheeks while his tongue raked her eyelids and nostrils like her aunt's dogs and his teeth pierced her neck, drawing blood. He tore open her coat and shredded her shirt so that her tiny breasts lapped the icy air. He pushed up her skirt and his hands seemed to split her in two as he clawed at her between her legs and forced his fingers up her as if he were trying to reach to the bottom of something. Then his hand closed around her throat until she couldn't breathe and he began dipping into her. She felt herself tearing open, like one of the frogs her brother ripped apart with a firecracker. When he was done he rose, spat, and pissed in the snow. Without looking her way, he buttoned up, got back into the car, slamming the door so hard that Ada feared she'd been shot. After he drove off, she lay on the ground a long while blinking at the stars, which blinked mildly back. When one streaked through the dark, she automatically shut her eyes to make a wish, but no words came. What she wanted she could not bring herself to wish for: she wanted that soldier dead.

At home she found her aunt asleep in the chair beside a spent fire. Ada crept past. If she ever found out what happened, her aunt would be furious. She shouldn't have gone out alone after dark. She ought to have stayed home. Her aunt had warned her about the soldiers.

She took the water pitcher and the basin out into the indigo night. The flat world was lacquered with milky blue ice. She stripped off her blouse, skirt, and the blood-dappled pantaloons, and shivered. They flapped in her fist as wind horses stormed the bristling white plain and she submerged them in water, which had already begun growing a peel. Her tears froze. She tried digging up the earth to bury the bloody clothes but the ground was hard as granite. A black goat ran up to her and rammed her with its clipped horns. Her hands began bleeding, so she quit and went inside.

Not wishing to disturb the dogs in her bed, she lay her blanket down on the floor, the bloody clothes rolled up under her head. Staring at the ceiling, she listened to her aunt snore. She wondered how her mother was faring back in the city. She missed her. Her mother would know how to make her feel better.

Brovko awoke and walked over to her. He sniffed her but when he tried licking her she automatically smacked his nose and the confused beast shuffled off back to her bed.

"Home late?" her aunt asked the next morning.

Ada, who hadn't slept at all, nodded, squinting her eyes to stop the tears. The old woman knew too much about trouble to press her.

"Well, don't worry, there's no time to think about your adventures. We have plenty of work to do," she said. She'd started the fire going and soon the house smelled of wood smoke.

Ada stepped outside and saw that it was morning. A bright sun scattered diamonds across the snow. No headstone of clouds marked the spot. Scornful chickens gathered around, demanding their due. At that moment she realized that the outside world cared what had happened to her about as much as the chickens did. For the rest of her life, she kept silent about it. Only a few people ever suspected there had been such a night. Over years, she buried it under layers of earth and air, distance and dreams, remembering it as merely the evening she'd gone skating one last time before all the ice was shattered by bombs.

But a boundary had been breached. After the rape, she could no longer contain her dreams. They began spilling out—every so often she'd hear a voice or see a person she'd dreamed about, leaving her unsure whether she was awake or asleep. She would see her grandfather, who'd also been a school teacher, standing at the blackboard, saying: "Dushko (which meant little soul), you know that the city was founded by three brothers. Unfortunately, they hated each other ..."

4

A letter from her father summoned her back to the city. Her mother was dying.

Walking home from the train station, heart pounding, Ada nervously eyed the German soldiers parading rifles.

The Ribbentrop-Molotov pact briefly allied the Soviets with the Germans, who proceeded to divide Eastern Europe between themselves. For a time, the communists of Voskresene were in power, and many of Ada's family's friends were arrested and either deported or executed. Among the nearly two million people who disappeared from the region in less than a year was Ada's brother, Viktor.

There were few neighbors you could trust because you were never certain who'd become a collaborator: in short order, the Germans attacked their allies. The blitzkrieg lasted four months. Retreating, the communists slaughtered their prisoners and everyone was sure Viktor was dead.

Some of the citizens welcomed the Germans into Voskresene,

believing they would treat them better than had the Russians. They helped their new masters. In the early days after their arrival a pogrom against the Jews left thousands dead. In its wake rumors circulated that the attack had been instigated by the communists. Others said the people had long wanted Jewish blood. In any case, before the year was out, across the country close to a million Jews had been murdered.

Most of the population remained skeptical about the Germans and the small group of partisans enlarged their enemies list by adding to it the names of the servants of the Reich. The Reich-skomissar said in a speech to his staff that his job was to suck up all the goods he could get. "If I find a native worthy of sitting at the same table with me," he said, "I shall have to have him shot." Himmler went further, proposing the "entire intelligentsia should be decimated." The circle of skeptics grew rapidly as the stateless citizens discovered just how *untermenschen* they were.

By the time she got there, Ada's brothers and sisters had already returned to the apartment and their presence made things oddly festive though the rooms reeked of stale sheets and sweat.

"We're vultures waiting for the deer to die," said Halia, the most morbid of her siblings.

They took turns sitting beside their mother, who tried her best to rally. She pointed at the family portrait hanging on the wall and asked Ada if she remembered the day it was made.

"I couldn't wait to get back to the sea," Ada said, nuzzling her face in her mother's hot neck.

When they weren't watching over her, the brothers and sisters clustered together in the living room. The twins played tug of war with a scarf until Edward let go and Hannusia tumbled over Christia who roared so loud Ada had to warn them to be quiet or they'd wake Mother.

Ada was sitting at the sill when she saw her father walking down the street in the company of four soldiers, several of whom carried rifles. They stopped in front of the building whose wooden door was ornamented with carved, inlaid panels. Ada tapped on the glass but they didn't hear her. She wanted to call out but the sash was stuck.

Then she heard herself scream: one of the soldiers smacked her father with his rifle butt. Dr. Sich sank to the ground. Ada's brothers and sisters turned toward her but she said no, there's nothing, just an old woman who fell, go back to playing. She glared at them so sternly, they obeyed. Meanwhile, she watched another soldier hoist a can over his head and douse her father with liquid. Her brothers and sisters watched Ada run out of the apartment, braid batting her back.

When she tried to claw her way over to her father, a stocky blond soldier blocked the door. She kicked him and scratched his neck. The soldier turned and hit her, once in the belly and once on the side of the head. Falling, she saw her father trying to rise. He staggered forward, then back. His screams drew others to the window and a crowd gathered around. Ada could hear her father but she couldn't get up. Blood gorged her eyes. She felt she was being pulled away by a powerful current. The crowd shouted and cursed but no one attacked the soldiers or tried to help because there was no one to call. The screaming grew louder. She struggled to her elbows and saw a huge flame dancing on the cobblestones. She hoped her brothers and sisters were not at the window. Then she dropped back down and shut her eyes. When she woke, the soldiers were gone but the smoldering body lay on the ground like an old log sprayed with sand. She shut her eyes again. Someone had moved it from the middle of the street so cars could get by. Her brother Vlodyk was hovering over her. It was hard to believe that no one had tried to help him, but she knew everyone was afraid.

She had no idea how impossible it would be to explain this to people who'd known only peace.

Ada was helped to her feet by a young man she didn't recognize.

"This is Lev," her brother said. "My friend from Scouts."

Panicked, Ada nodded, brushing her dress.

"Let me help," said Lev Kruk.

She stared at him. Then she began to sob. She crumpled back to the ground.

"Stay with her," Lev instructed Ada's brother. "I'll call some people."

And he did. Lev arranged everything. He knew where to find a reliable doctor, what to do with the body, and he even offered to speak to her mother.

The church, which had been boarded during the previous occupation, had not been reopened and it wasn't possible to hold a funeral. The remains, which rattled around the cloth bag Lev had brought, were taken directly to the cemetery where Lev managed to hunt up a few men to dig the grave. The soldiers had arrested most of the priests and it was difficult to find one, but finally Father Stus came forward on his own and performed the ceremony while Dr. Irene Buk, pale and coughing, her children, Lev, and Anton looked on, stunned, in the candle-lit dark. Throughout the service the children kept thinking of the wolves they heard lived in the cemetery, and when a dog barked Orest began whimpering. They were glad to get home.

Ada stared at the portrait in her mother's bedroom. So recently life had seemed normal. What had they done in the meantime to deserve this? Nothing. They had not done anything. She wouldn't accept blame for the evil actions of others. And what would they do with their father's clothes? These suits and shirts lined up in the closet, the trousers and socks in the drawers. The day before they had been necessities. If in fact they were not necessities but merely useless props, what then, besides food, did people really need? What was this freedom for which men were slaughtering each other?

A week later, Ada's mother died. Ada was sitting beside her as she slipped away, saying to herself, Mother you must stay here to help us, you can't leave us alone. Her mother's thin hair was matted and her skin was covered with pink splotches. Ada gripped her mother's hand and stared into her eyes as the light slowly left them. She could see it going but not where it was going. In the last seconds Ada felt it was as useless for her to struggle against death as it had been for her to fight the soldier who raped her. Time was a man. It was evening and the lamps outside had just gone on.

Lev was waiting with Father Stus in her living room. They buried her that same night beside her husband. "The cemetery's starting to feel like our living room," Ada said. An owl in the oak studied the service, sounding twice, causing the mourners to wonder. On the way home Lev took the lead and Ada brought up the rear, with the other children walking single file between them. The sound of their feet echoed through the empty streets. Her mind was heavy and dark and she wasn't sure what she would say to her younger siblings to comfort them. Clearly parents were not permanent fixtures, but she found herself unable to accept their disappearance. She would not let them go, she told herself. She would pursue them beyond the gates of death.

Luckily, war left no room for mourning or introspection. While everyone lay in bed, Lev and Ada sat silently, side by side, on the sofa in the living room. Ada was now head of the family and the responsibility matured her overnight. Her voice grew firmer. She feared her hair would turn gray. She rested her head on Lev's shoulder and put her hand over his. Both fell into a light sleep sitting on the couch.

Just before dawn, as the pigeons began their begging rounds, they were wakened by a knock. Lev shot up, reaching for the folding knife he carried in his pocket. Silently, he and Ada rose and walked down the corridor together.

Lev threw open the door.

Standing there were two young men Ada's age, both tall, a little stooped, with flat black hair pasted down tightly around their skulls. Their hands were at their sides and their heads pointed down. One glanced up quickly at Ada, then dropped his gaze to the floor, as though he were addressing the threshold.

"Baruch. Seth," Ada said, startled. The twins had been students of her mothers' in grade school. Ada had gotten to know them when the family lived in the Jewish quarter some years earlier.

Lev asked Ada what she wanted to do and she replied, "Let them in."

"They're Jews," Lev said.

"I know them," Ada answered.

Inside, the two boys stood around awkwardly until she practically shoved them into the living room.

"What happened?"

"They shot our father. Our mother's disappeared."

"Mine too."

Their eyes mirrored their disbelief.

While Ada had heard about the Jewish ghetto, she never quite understood the prejudices. She didn't really get what a Jew was. She knew they didn't go to church and didn't even believe in Jesus—yet, even though her family several times celebrated Yom Kippur with the Ghitelmans, or maybe precisely because of this, there was something about the distinction between humans that didn't make sense to her. Jew? Christian? Moslem? Two legs two eyes two hands, some brains, or maybe not. And while she heard the men at her father's table refer to Jews, sometimes with enthusiasm, other times with hostility, her heart never grasped what her ears heard.

"They'll kill you if they find out we're here," said Seth, who'd clearly taken time dressing himself. Ada noticed how shiny his shoes were.

"But they'll never know," added his brother.

"That's not necessarily so," said Seth.

"You going to tell them?" Baruch argued.

The brothers went back and forth. Lev stood at the window, staring down the street. Finally he said:

"I have to go out. How long will you stay?"

"A couple of days. We have an uncle outside of town. He'll help us."

"How will you get there?"

The boys felt Lev's skepticism and a note of caution came into their voices.

"We'll find a way." Seth answered and Baruch nodded.

Lev looked at Ada and said:

"Keep everyone home. No one will be surprised if they don't see you for a few days. I'll be back Friday."

He leaned toward Ada as if to kiss her but she drew away. Lev shrugged and moved to the door. A centipede crawled along the wall and Lev smashed it with the heel of his palm.

Seth, Baruch, and Ada sat silently in the living room until the sun came up and they heard the kids stirring in the next room.

"What will you tell them?" Seth asked.

Ada was surprised at her answer, which was in line with the way life unfolded: the stranger the situation, the easier it felt. Nothing was like what she had imagined it would be, not her mother's death, or her father's absence, or knowing what she risked by having these two stay. It was as if reality were playing a game, trying to keep her at a distance with vivid but illusory prejudices. In fact reality, no matter how dreadful, almost always felt better than the fears she experienced trying to avoid it.

Quite likely, she was in shock, her heart hiding from the incessant assaults.

"You're mother's friends. Besides, I'm not letting them out for a couple of days," she said firmly.

Baruch stared at her calmly.

"You're pale as milk, girl. You should get some sleep."

Orko padded into the room.

"Who's that?"

"My name is Baruch, and I am a great wizard," Baruch replied as though saying "Good Morning."

Orko turned and ran back to the room.

Seth and Baruch lived with them for several days until, relying on a network unfamiliar to Ada, they arranged a way of escape.

"If we survive the war, we'll send you a postcard," Seth said.

Ada smiled. The whole experience sometimes felt like a game. It was only when someone was hurt that the stakes became vivid again. And yet this too was often hard to grasp in the moment—she could not, for example, believe that she would never see her parents again. Surely they would walk through the door at any minute, arms open in greeting.

Her grief found no place to grow and mundane chores kept her focused: Ada now had her brothers and sisters to care for. That may have been one reason why when he put his arms around her and kissed her, she no longer pushed Lev away.

It wasn't the only reason.

Though short, Lev was handsome, with a hooked nose and nervous blue eyes. He had the confidence of a much older man. He'd been with the partisans since his parents were dragged from the family farm and executed when he was fifteen and he'd grown up taking care of himself. For all of that, he had a broad romantic streak. War was the only thing he knew and he found its demands electrifying. Each moment revealed just how much he had to give, and it pleased him to extend his protectorate to Ada.

Yet he rarely confided in her: he never admitted that he was behind the assassination of the soldiers who killed her father. In fact, he never shared the details of any of his paramilitary work and this penchant for secrecy, along with his temper, slowly marked out a distance between them.

As the war dragged on, they talked more and more often about leaving the city. They couldn't stay: when the communists returned, they would certainly be executed. They were in constant danger from the Germans.

A surprise visit from the police one morning asking for Lev decided them. That evening, the family sorted out the essentials, stuffed them into two rucksacks, and headed out for the displaced persons camps being set up in territories where the war had already been won.

5

The displaced persons camps set up after the war by the International Relief Agency were models of efficiency that provided millions with the first stability they'd known in years. Children were born in the camps; funerals were held; votes taken; classes conducted; dreams refined and deferred. Love too found a home within the makeshift structures that, for many of its residents, clarified forever the differences between luxury and necessity.

In the camp one evening, standing in line waiting for dinner, tin dish in hand, Ada spotted a gypsy whose white beard was so long he parted it and draped the two strands over his shoulders like braids. She recognized the driver from the Crimea who had taken her family to the train station. She even remembered his story about Genghis Khan.

She noticed how milky white his eyes were. He was blind. His walking stick was a cane.

She loved baked potatoes and she always shepherded her brothers and sisters into line early, while the pots were still heaped high. Holding her face above the steaming spud she felt herself being dissolved in the hot fruits of the earth. Pressing down with her tin fork was like sinking into the burning sand of the beach.The hot meal scorched her tongue and she smiled to think of how little the sting bothered her. Perhaps this should have been a warning—that pain was becoming a seasoning without which things tasted too bland. For a moment she forgot about her brothers and sisters, heaven and hell, and the enormous questions ahead. If only she could sit like this forever she would count herself blessed among women.

"Are you Adriana Sich?" She opened her eyes. Before her stood a redhead whose face looked familiar—a common sensation in the camps. The woman wore a flowered print dress.

Ada nodded.

"I just wanted to tell you your father was a great man. You should have this." The woman leaned over, handed her an envelope, and walked away.

Strange. Ada studied her swift motions as the redhead heaved out of the commissary.

"Who was that?" asked Orest.

Ada ignored him. Inside the envelope was a gold bracelet that she weighed in her hand, finding it neither particularly heavy nor especially elegant. Then she remembered the woman: the naked redhead on the beach at the Black Sea. She hadn't thought of her in years. And while she was hardly surprised that her parents had a past and a history, she felt a pang—she would never be sure who they had been.

"Excuse me, please, may I talk to you for one minute?" a woman's voice lisped at her.

Ada, who'd been smoking outside the mess hall, waiting for Lev to return from his soccer match, looked at the woman in the brown tailored business suit holding a pencil and pad. She also wore a green eye patch.

Ada and Lev had been studying English and she was pleased she'd understood the question, yet she was quite nervous.

"Sorry but I do not speak English good. What is to your eye?" Now that she had more time she found herself poring over magazines like *Life* and reading not only favorites such as Stefan Zweig and Franz Werfel, but also writers like Orwell, whose book *Animal Farm* had been translated into Ukrainian by a friend of hers, though she herself had preferred the original.

"Conjunctivitis," said the woman. Somehow the lisp and eye patch relieved Ada. The Americans at least tried to be friendly.

"OK."

"I'm doing a story on life in the camps." Her teeth were so straight. "Could you tell our readers what it's like for a refugee?"

She hadn't really objectified herself yet, though eventually she'd find it hard to see herself any other way.

She sucked on her Lucky Strike and thought a while. Then she said:

"When so many people you know died, it's not the same world. You live in different place."

"What is the best you can hope for now?" the journalist asked.

Again Ada tried smiling.

"You see, I leave many things in my house but they are not important. Being near my family. That. Yes?"

Walking alone through the woods outside the camp, listening to birds singing their hearts out, as though the world were young, Ada made some resolutions. She was vaguely conscious of an angry voice demanding vengeance, which she fought to keep down. Instead, she concentrated on keeping herself as open as possible. She would envy no one. Wherever she went from here she would be at a disadvantage, surrounded by people bound to each other in that web of past actions called history.

"Very wise," said her father. She imagined him leaning on a rock, dressed in his long black coat and fine felt hat, his chin balanced on the handle of an umbrella.

She was startled by the clarity of the apparition. He smiled and said:

"It isn't easy to make myself visible, so don't expect it too often."

"Is mother there with you?"

"Certainly. I believe she's visiting Hannusia. There are quite a few of you, you know. Do you want me to call her?"

"Still left, you mean."

He winced at the reproach.

"You're angry."

"You slipped away a little early, wouldn't you say? Do you think you'd taught me everything I need?"

"As to that, yes. Your mother and I provided you with an excellent guide to the invisible world."

"And where is that? I'm afraid most of us are still very much in the visible one."

"Commandments, for one. Don't be arrogant. You think Death is simple? Just: here, then gone? Listen, Death is every bit as difficult as life."

Such imaginary conversations helped her. Talking with her ghosts made her feel less angry and alone.

Around her, the maples were in their autumn beauty. She picked up a leaf and ran her fingers along its veins. Every year the trees lost everything too and each spring they returned.

Descending the mountain down a road shaded by riotous canopies, she ran into Anton who was waving excitedly.

He'd grown a mustache and a goatee and looked a little too much like Lenin for Ada's taste. He'd become a scholar who sat up all night wherever he could find a light, reading poetry and studying the mystical treatises of Jacob Boehme and the Kabbala.

Anton made friends easily and his circle soon included a number of American soldiers, including a young lieutenant named Tom O'Flannagan. Tall, even elegant, with close-cropped peach-colored hair, the soldier had just begun his career teaching history at American University when the war broke out. His own father, an immigrant from County Cork, had urged him to fullfill his duty and enlist. A veteran of Normandy, he'd seen enough, he told Anton, to have his sense of history enlarged in a way that no amount of reading could ever have done. And while he hoped he'd learned lessons he'd bear in mind for life, he feared it wouldn't be long before he would begin to forget. Lieutenant O'Flannagan was especially eager to offer the future émigrés his insights about what to expect in America. He and Fedko and

Anton, whom he called Dostoevsky Junior, and a few others sometimes sat around the mess hall for hours, talking. Occasionally Ada lingered. The scene reminded her of dinners at her father's table.

"But America isn't a nation," Fedko argued. "It's a club. I mean, look at us: with a little luck we're going to become Americans without having been born inside its borders."

O'Flannagan prickled.

"You'll see. It really is a nation even though citizenship requirements don't include being born there. Old definitions have been rewritten. You don't need to spring from the soil to be a native. Blue blood buys no better beer than red."

"Really?" Fedko challenged him. "You're saying there's no aristocracy? I wonder. I mean, the difference between the Russian Revolution and the American one, is that yours was led by your upper classes instead of against them. Which, I may say, is why it worked out. But I have a question for you."

"Shoot."

"Where's the power? Who really has power in America?"

The question was on the mind of every immigrant-to-be.

O'Flannagan tapped out a Lucky Strike and offered cigarettes all around. Everyone smoked, including Ada. He loved the feel of the classroom and sensed himself slowly making the tranistion from warrior back to citizen.

"Where's the power? Numbers. Numbers rule ..."

"Money. I know," Fedko said.

"Well, in some ways, but it's not that simple. There's also public opinion, the people.

"I'm going to England," Anton said. "Things are clearer there. It's still Europe."

"England's going to be pretty tough right now," said Fedko.

"And that's good. America's going to be even rougher," Anton answered.

"Why do you say that?" O'Flannagan asked.

"Because it won. It's discovered incredible power. And liberty and power are always at war. That's what the story of Christ is about, I think. Christ represents total *spiritual* liberty, which appears as creativity. By reminding individuals of the nearly infinite power within, you show the limits of external authority. And that's a threat to those whose power, no matter how widespread their influence may appear, has been so reduced it relies on coercion. Watch out for people so corrupted they run from the mirror of art because it threatens their self-delusions."

"Watch out for self-deluded artists," quipped Fedko.

O'Flannagan smiled again:

"Hey, Dostoevsky Junior. I love how you people get off on this kind of talk. But enough for me. Movie in a minute."

"What is it?" Anton asked.

" *To Have and Have Not.* "

"Hemingway. Read it?"

"Can't say. Heard of it."

"Not his best."

Anton was always reading, Ada thought as she watched him approach, his hands bouncing like springs at his sides.

"Ada! They accepted me. I'm going!"

"Who?"

"The University of London. I'm going to study in England." His nineteen-year-old exuberance made her laugh.

"Do you think T. S. Eliot is still alive? I haven't seen a literary journal in over a year."

Ada shook her head. Who?

"Oh, look, a fox!"

Ada turned and saw the red-headed creature slipping off into the bushes.

Then she threw her arms around Anton and dappled his face with kisses. Friendly kisses, to be sure, but they reminded her of the more than friendly ones she had recently given Lev, who had asked her to marry him, and she shivered and pulled abruptly away from the bewildered poet, whose passion for Ada was as clear as the outlines of the ancient trees falling on the road ahead—bare, ruined choirs where late the sweet birds sang.

Ada had no idea of the effect she had on the poet. He had lost both his parents and his sister to the war. He would wait, vainly as it turned out, a lifetime for a moment of similar intensity. The day he left his country the door closed on the sources of his poetry. This didn't have to be the case—émigrés always brought up the example of Viktor Hugo, who did his best work in exile. But Anton was not that kind of a writer. He believed, sentimentally, that true poetry was written in the language your grandmother loved you in, and that language would now be lost to him. For the rest of his life he rationalized his silence by telling himself that, had Ada's embrace been passionate rather than comradely, he might have found a muse. Instead, he had to settle for literary criticism.

It was around this time Ada established her embassy: she remained on good terms with the dead. At one time or another, every one of her deceased family members appeared before her. She was especially close to Nina, the last-born of her mother's children, who fled when only a few hours old. Nina's swift translation from the material world to the ethereal sphere gave her prerogatives among the dead, and she worked energetically on behalf of her sister as Ada struggled to find her place in the new world. She appeared to Adriana as a floating husk of green, a pine cone limned by colored light.

6

Ada's upper body rippled like a leafy tree on which a thousand birds had settled. She was sitting up in bed, propped by three feather pillows sheathed in decade-old pink cases. The ripples turned to tremors, and all the leaves began falling at once: she was sobbing. She had just read the story of her life. She'd been certain that she would never again meet anyone who knew her past, that she was destined to live in a universe where people without common roots showed each other only surfaces, a brittle sensation robbing life of its sustaining warmth. For once she didn't stop herself, didn't try being brave, or denying all she had seen, all that had happened to her. Her body had held the grief so long that now she finally acknowledged it, it was as though someone had thrown open all the gates of an over-crowded prison: every part of her shook with feelings too long confined, a riot of inmates dancing in a deluge of tears.

Later, her still slim body wrung dry, she lay stretched out on her bed, head on pillow, and thought about what she had read. It was not exactly her story, of course. Anton had changed things: he had to, he hadn't been there to see most of it, after all. Her father had not been doused with gasoline and set on fire before her eyes: he had been arrested with a group of friends and thrown alive into an open grave where he had been covered with lime. She never saw his body and had no idea where it was buried. There had been no Seth and Baruch—their names had been Edko and Olka, former neighbors. She'd received a letter from Israel telling her they had reached it safely back in 1947 while she was still in the displaced persons camp. After that she lost touch with them. As to the ghosts—that was true, she did speak to the dead more than she cared to admit, but how did Anton know?

Poets.

Bits of what she had just read flashed through her mind like shards of a dream. Anton's images seemed more powerful than her own memories. Suddenly she couldn't recall whether Slava had ever been seized by a tornado or whether or not she had visited a monastery with her father. How was it possible that the things Anton imagined could displace what had really happened?

She looked at the clock by her bed: after four. In a couple of hours she would have to get her boys up for school—though God knows they were old enough to do it themselves.

They were growing away from her. For years now they'd refused to speak Ukrainian, insisting on English. Understanding their choice did not make it any easier to surrender to it. Her job was to be a bridge between worlds, but so far it looked like the traffic sped in only one direction.

And yet here was Anton's story: what was it if not an attempt to redeem the past? Suddenly she felt very tired. She closed her eyes. Images of her mother as she remembered her from life melted into the mother in Anton's tale and a composite appeared to take Ada by the hand and lead her down the sea. For the first time in years, Ada slept deeply.

7

All that week Ada thought about Anton's proposal. Vacuuming the apartment, she tried imagining what it might be like to take herself and her fatherless sons to England. What really held her here? Why should she stay? She had estranged the community. The boys were growing wild. Her job was boredom incarnate. When her looks went, she'd be as invisble as hotel furniture. Why not surrender to an unexpected romance?

Over the next days, her future clarified itself as surely as though her intrusive dead had choired: Albion will save you, fly to Albion! What a fool, to think she'd survive America, where the race was to the swiftest and the richest. She needed an ordered society where everything was in its place—in such a country a place might also be found for her. Above all she needed help with her sons. Someone like Anton, skilled and purposeful, could give the boys a sense of tradition and open the gates of the future a little.

Late one evening she mentioned the possibility to Viktor who, to her surprise, shook his head.

"To England? You know how they'd treat you? Ada," he said.

"Anton has a good job."

"Enough to support you and your sons? And them? Their school, their lives? How would it be for them?" Viktor said anxiously, drawing on his cigarette.

They were sitting in the kitchen, over the bathtub above which hung a cloud of smoke. A dish of radish tops lay alongside the half-empty bottle of Vodka.

She did not, as a rule, consult Viktor. He led a shadowy life of which Ada remained, by choice, only dimly aware.

Yes, Viktor the Spinner had become a complication. His presence might have simplified things: he could have become the economic and psychological support Ada needed. Instead, he was another drain.

Released from Siberia in the early fifties, during a May Day amnesty, he somehow managed to track down his sister, which amazed Ada because Viktor seemed best at getting lost. First he went looking for sugar and got lost for fifteen years. In America, he got lost the first time he went to New York by himself; and he got lost his second day at the brewery and had to wait for the foreman to find him again. He lost job after job. He strangled inside his own thoughts. When he looked in the mirror he saw blue eyes and a face with clean lines and blond hair that, to his surprise, hadn't gone white. He lost himself in rage, with never a clear object for his anger, except of course for the enemy in the old country. No one cared about them anymore, so he kept the searing feelings to himself. When his anger grew too intense, he'd get up and spin, his mind a battlefield of knives, blood, cut limbs.

He returned over and over to the morning his life changed:

outside it was cold and gray; inside, the cat sat on the kitchen table, licking a paw while Adriana leaned against the stove, reading. He was off to meet his friend Vlad. Together they were going to cross the border. Instead, when he arrived at the designated meeting area, three policemen were already waiting. They told him Vlad had left—and then they arrested him. He never heard from his high school classmate again. Instead he roomed with spiders the size of softballs and never saw his parents alive again.

In prison he was penetrated more often than a pin cushion, and now the only time he was found was when he had something inside him, something huge, hot or cold; he liked metal, gun barrels, but these were rare (yet good to find), so let others think he was lost; he knew where he was going. Tim, who had a tattoo parlor in the port, showed him Newark and New York, and soon Viktor had friends everywhere. They were playful and violent and death studied their games, waiting to see how far they would go, and they went far, because screaming was good.

He watched over his sister's sons reluctantly. He knew his was not a healthy gaze. He showed them his Museum of the Horrors of History. For years he'd been collecting pictures. A few came from the magazines under his bed; others were death camp photos; one or two were from the Famine. There was one of a boy's naked body, his penis lopped off, that echoed in his mind when he tried sleeping. He thought of removing it from the wall but then he decided it was more important to remember than to sleep. Best of all, of course, was the 80 percent solution called vodka.

Ada waited for him to heal. She hoped that one day he would awaken as himself again, but it never happened. In the camp in Vorkutah his ass had to be resown because it had split from too much hammering and his shit wouldn't stay in. During an interrogation, he'd seen a detective bring in a bucket of eyeballs and heap a fistful on the table. Using a pistol butt, he shattered them like eggs. He swept the ooze into a pan with his open palm, held it over a Bunsen burner, then spoon-fed the fried eyes to a prisoner, not him, thank God. As for God. Viktor loved glory holes and dungeons and rest stops after dark. It didn't occur to him that darkness wasn't necessary.

When he heard Ada was thinking of going to England, he panicked.

The next morning when he wasn't at breakfast, Ada went to his room to see whether he was asleep and found his bed made but she didn't think much of it because every so often Viktor disappeared for a day.

When he still wasn't back the next morning, she began worrying. She phoned my mother, who in turn called my father at the hospital, and he promised that if Viktor weren't back soon he'd go looking for him.

She peered into his room at the grim pictures on the walls, and shuddered. The buzz of the bell brought her back to the present and she hurried to open it.

"Anton!" In the anxiety of the morning she'd forgotten that he was coming back.

Above his neatly knotted tie, his lean, thought-marked face stared hopefully into hers.

"Come in," she said.

He'd barely stepped over the threshhold when she began:

"I loved that painter. I remember him. The Opera House. Mother and father. I felt them."

They walked side by side into the kitchen.

"You're not coming," he said, slipping his hands into his jacket, his shoulders sagging a bit.

"I want to come. I want to come," she said. "Coffee?" His heart was beating quickly. She didn't want to have to decide. She wanted to go yet she couldn't imagine beginning again. At least here the troubles were by now familiar, Fear whispered.

"No. You should come. What's here for you? What's here?"

"It's Viktor," her voice angry. "Viktor's missing. He's disappeared. Not the first time, but when he's gone more than a day I feel it's 1942 again."

Anton looked concerned.

"I've called Slava."

"I'm sure he's alright."

"Probably, probably; my nerves certainly aren't. Why couldn't he pick some other time?"

"Can I help? You've got to come," he said, surprised by his own desperation. What use was literature if it didn't move people to action?

His slim body tightened. He would be an arrow. He would pierce her heart.

She came up to him and put her hand on his. At an age when most women settle into second chins, he thought, she grew more attractive, as though she'd arrived late into her own body, its resistance to gravity impressive. Her skin was hardly wrinkled and her eyes burned with a complex light.

"How few people are willing to say even that," she said.

"Little people."

"I can't. Not now. When are you leaving?"

Her resolve deepened with every word, even as she knew she was making a mistake, closing a door that might have opened on freedom.

"Tomorrow. But that doesn't matter. You can come later."

"Maybe," she said, thinking: *Who knows?*

She leaned over and kissed him. It began idly, a parting gift, and turned richer.

While she appeared solid and fixed from the outside, inwardly Ada was aflutter, kiting in the winds of the moment. Anton, meanwhile, seemed to have disappeared. She wanted him to touch her, push her down, taker her; instead, he leaned back and gazed at her with a hurt look.

"I don't have anybody to talk to," he said. "Nobody understands what I've seen."

The streets and smells of a hundred days gathered around him like a cloud, and she stared at him, confused, certain she was making a mistake, but unable to extricate herself from the vise of the moment. Just as when she was a girl, she felt trapped by her family, her life again ruined by her brother, whose previous disappearance had partly broken her mother. We repeat ourselves, she thought; we repeat ourselves. That is our tragedy.

After Anton left, she stood in the kitchen looking out the window while her mind cast forth images from the past alongside fantasies about the future. Just as during the war, she had no time for reflection. Had to get to work, where she gratefully lost herself in the customers' demands, all of which she was able to satisfy.

That evening she came home late to find her sons huddled around the television. Still no Viktor.

She passed another bad night. Unable to sleep, she finally dozed near morning and was startled awake by the bell.

She found Alex already at the door. Beside him stood a still-drunken Viktor, accompanied by my father and me.

Saying he wanted me to feel at home everywhere, Father often took me on jobs or errands to unusual neighborhoods.

He'd made some calls and had, without too much difficulty, found out where Viktor was. Early that Saturday, we got into his green Volkswagen beetle and set off for Newark.

Some years ago, for obvious reasons, I grew interested in the Russian Revolution. I quickly discovered how ignorant I was on the subject. For instance, it's arguable that the revolution was kicked off by Father Gapon in 1905. Son of peasants, the priest believed Christ's message had practical applications for the workers of St. Petersburg. He lived with them, tasted their misery, and hastened to their needs. The distance between the rich and the poor was wild as ever. One branch of Russia's royal family owned a hundred and fifty miles of beach frontage, and on holidays mountains made popular presents. Victoria and the Kaiser had done the same, swapping hills in Africa. Workers, meanwhile, lived in shacks without power or furniture. Eight people crowded into a dark room where the winter temperature could fall below zero. Romans treated their slaves better. Gapon was outraged. He spoke passionately. Workers trusted him. Unlike many priests of the day, he was thin and ascetic and wasn't looking for ways to grow rich off the sweat of the poor. The secret police also liked him because he was honest and they supported him. Despite his demands for improvements in working conditions, however, nothing happened, so the workers decided to stage a march in St. Petersburg, which Gapon was responsible for coordinating. Following months of strikes by nearly every sector of the city's services, St. Petersburg was without power or public transportation; curfews were in place.

On Sunday, before dawn, the workers started gathering by the tens of thousands. They'd been told that certain streets were off limits—don't disturb the rich. Gapon ignored the restrictions. One group marched on the Czar's Winter Palace, where they were attacked by police working with the army. Hundreds were killed. Gapon himself fled the country. His autobiography, *My Confession*, was published in the United States in 1907. When he returned to St. Petersburg, he was assassinated either by a police agent or a Social Revolutionary whom, incidentally, a Russian sly-boots writer by the name of Sirin claimed to have met in the home of the wealthy émigré Fondaminsky in Paris in 1936, commenting on the red freckles covering the hands with which the agent allegedly strangled the priest. In any case, the Russian Revolution had started. It was the Russian Revolution, of course, which in part led us to Vietnam, that death, those tears. Because of Father Gapon, my father and I found ourselves driving through the slums of Newark in the VW, looking for Mr. Enko's house.

In the 1860s, Newark had been the leading industrial city in America. Before that, it had been called the most beautiful town on the continent. Plastic had been developed here. A century later, the summer of 1967, after Martin Luther King was assassinated, riots broke out. Drugs had been flowing into the city for a while. The father of a friend, who worked in a garage in Newark's Iron-bound district, was on his way to work one morning. At a light, five men came up to his car and before he could get away they pulled him out and began beating him. He was a large, strong man who'd been an athlete in school and he fought back, which made the beating worse. He might have been killed had a police car not come by, siren wailing. The men dropped him and ran. He was sent to the hospital for stitches, after which he went to the garage, worked an extra shift, and then came home. The next day the city was on fire, and the garage where he worked was burned down. It took him several months to find another job, during which period he and his wife fought intensely and the relationship deteriorated beyond repair. These were the American wars.

Newark had once been the city of poets. Stephen Crane had been born here. Whitman had walked these streets. The houses looked in bad shape but there were also new developments that made one think things could improve if people really wanted it.

A black, three-legged lab hobbled along the gutter. A lot next door looked like the site of a surreal yard sale of exploded green chairs, boxes of empty cans, and a tower of tires. A Volvo lay in the middle of the yard on its roof like a beetle or a dog waiting for someone to come by and scratch its belly.

We were headed for Walter Enko's. Walter had been a deacon at the church for a time and now, in his mid-sixties, he worked as a travel agent. His flat bald head reminded me of a mushroom. His eyes were slanted—Tartar blood. He appeared at the door wearing an orange sweat suit.

We all shook hands. He looked both distressed and relieved to see us. Father quickly made some joke to put him at his ease.

"Please come," Mr. Enko rasped, "He's upstairs."

We followed him up the dark stairwell. Most of the paint had peeled off and the bare plaster was covered with graffiti. The place smelled of decayed meat and outside an apartment on the first landing we saw hardened dog turds.

We entered into the living room, where we found Viktor lying on the sofa, awake but still as a stone.

He wore gray wool trousers and a cream-colored shirt stained with green across the front. His skin was tight over the bone, cheeks sharp as teeth. He breathed heavily through his mouth, and every few minutes his tongue darted out like a thirsty dog's. His red eyes blinked at us, showing no signs of recognition. His gray beard was spangled with shreds of bread and flakes of food.

"He's still a little out of it. He came to me like this last night."

Mr. Enko gestured at the nearly empty bottle of vodka standing open on the brown carpet near the lacquered pine coffee table.

"Mr. Enko, will you help me get him down to the car?" Father asked.

"Yes, of course, but first can I give you some coffee?"

"Thank you, Mr. Enko."

"Drink?"

"We should just get him in a car and go home."

"I don't blame you. You know, it's not the first time he came here like this."

"Really? Does Ada know?"

"No, of course she doesn't. She's one of those determinators."

"What?"

"She decides what everyone should do and how they should be, and that's that. If they're not like that, they should be."

"What's he do here?"

"Coffee?" He was pleading.

"A little water," Father finally broke down. We followed Walter into the kitchen. The walls were peeling and the ceiling looked like shale. Slats of wood peered through the plaster. The sink brimmed with dishes caked with grease and burnt potatoes. Plates towered on the counters and kitchen table. I counted three open cans of peaches, and several of corn and peas. A dish of milk on the floor beside the refrigerator had a roach in it.

"I am not good at homework."

"Me neither."

Somehow Mr. Enko was able to find three unused glasses. He turned on the tap.

"Don't mind the color."

The water was a pale orange.

Father drank it as though it were champagne, smacking his lips all the way.

Back in the living room, Viktor had managed to sit up. He stared vaguely at me.

Mr. Enko's husky voice flickered softly.

"You see, Mr. Peter. It's the community. They wouldn't understand. But a doctor. You know human beings. "

He smiled awkwardly at my father.

I stood there, eyes fixed on the shadow of the curtain against the dirt-brown rug.

"This is the only place where he can be himself. Here, he's funny. Never stops telling jokes. Some of them about his sister."

It was hard for me to imagine Viktor in a light mood.

The two were lovers—or as close as they could come to it. I sensed it then, and know it now. Viktor had been here all along. Walter was lying to us, and would continue to lie, and that was all right, he didn't have much choice, there was no easy way for him to tell the truth about his life—the community wouldn't allow it. The immigrants wanted to show the mainstream a certain face—tie-wearing, married, mortgage-paying, little leaguers. They didn't have the confidence to show themselves; they feared what they felt was their darkness.

Father helped Viktor down the stairs, while I opened doors. It was warm and the radio promised rain.

Sometimes I forget I am imagining this.

"I want to go home," Adriana said.

We had put Viktor to bed and were again in the kitchen.

Alex could barely look at me.

"I want to go home," Ada repeated in Father's direction. "Enough. I'm going back. As soon as Viktor wakes up."

"Adriana."

Her eyes shut in long parentheses. She leaned back against the wall and tilted her blond head to the ceiling, hands balled in fists at her sides. Not impossible. She could take Viktor; or maybe he'd move in with Mr. Enko.

We left awkwardly and I regretted having accompanied Father. Alex wouldn't forgive me too easily.

That night, driving back to the comfortable suburbs of Fort Hills, where we'd moved the year before, I brooded over forking destinies. Conventional wisdom calls hard luck a school for character. But when you start asking just who the scholars so comfortable in their judgments are, you find their experiences would strike an Ada as comic relief; and their authority would pale beside the silent wisdom lodged within the bodies and the hearts of lambs whose throats have been slit only part of the way.

8

A memory: I am awakened by a noise that turns out to be my gerbil Squeezy whirling his wheel—the very one who, soon after, will flee his cage and hide behind a door I will throw open in my search for him (so Squeezy will get squozed). This night, however, he is safe.

Unable to get back to sleep, I sit up. It is midnight. The window's darkness draws me. I pad over and stare out. Instead of stars, I see the panes of neighbors, black rectangles lit by street lamps below which hulk the scarab shells of cars, enamel agleam. And there's Pietro, still pacing. I don't know who he's dressed as. His neck swivels side to side—he's looking for someone to harass, but the street is empty, so he keeps his demons to himself. Beyond, the sleepy sea of houses. Some smaller, some taller. At this moment they even look like waves. It comforts me to no end to imagine someone there, up late, having similar thoughts. One day we'll meet, go to football games, eat hot dogs, ride bicycles, become friends. Or maybe it's a girl, heart ashiver with yearning: we'll fall in love, have children. I turn away certain that deep within the raw, democratic darkness dwell new friends, a future, my fate.

Heading for the refrigerator, I pass the bedroom, hear my mother's snore behind the half-closed door. On the threshold of the kitchen, I pause. The light above the table is on. Half-hidden behind a high-rise of textbooks hunches Father, hand to forehead. The other hand clutches a pen with which he laboriously copies out brontosaurus-sized words explaining in plain Latin what we are made of. I can almost see him whispering "metatarsal" to himself, identifying that part of the foot from which the blood flows on a stigmatic—though of course he doesn't think of that—and I am no longer that boy stirred from sleep by a gerbil spinning in a wheel but a middle-aged man looking down the corridor of memory at one image out of a million. But the significance of that picture of Father impresses me as much now as it did then—a man alone leaning into the world of knowledge hidden inside a book. The fact that it was contained, that the words were fixed in their places by type set and broken up long ago, explains part of the source of its authority. If it was in a book, it had to be important. Words that described nothing more than the organs and muscles and veins of the body. His knowledge of it, born of his attention to the book, was slowly, imperceptibly, invisibly laying a road out for us—away from this neighborhood of triple deckers, of people warm and troubled, loud and full of tears, to a new home, with a yard surrounded by a fence, eventually a dog and two cars, in the upper-middle-class suburb of Fort Hills, home to CPAs, doctors, lawyers, and other types skilled at skinning the poor.

We prospered. And no doubt one of the reasons we moved was to put some distance between us and the Kruks.

The flip side to my mother's apparently successful integration into her new life as an American doctor's wife was her unwillingness to talk about the past. Unwillingness may be too strong, because I can't say that at sixteen I was especially curious about it. Everyone is given their time: it is the one common gift. Why should we covet anyone else's or struggle to preserve what wisdom tells us can be held about as readily as light itself? In those years my parents accepted the challenges of the moment, hurling themselves into responsibilities—work, social life—so anxiously they hardly noticed how little time we saved for each other. In Roosevelt I'd gone to Catholic School and attended Saturday classes where I learned about the old country; in Fort Hills I switched to public school, with its emphasis on sports and college prep, and the old country, which had seemed abstract enough already, faded like the Cheshire cat, leaving only an enigmatic grin. For years the past's grim smile sat on a shelf, nearly invisible, though never quite gone.

Eventually we even stopped coming down for Mass, signing on to the local Catholic Church instead, where only mother became a regular parishoner while Father and I drifted into a not altogether comfortable apostasy. At least it felt uneasy to me—I won't speak for Father. He was a practical man and we never broached such ineffables. For me, something has lingered, a strong sense that there is more to our experiences than our senses can say. It is this intimation that gives me whatever I know of hope.

School work absorbed me; I began playing tennis. But, perhaps because my parents took the job of assimilation so seriously, I found myself adopting a more laid back approach. I was slow to make new friends. And, while I did well academically, I missed the noises of the old streets, which were never without people, and, more and more, I found that I missed the Kruks.

Alex hadn't wanted me to leave. He called often yet he never once came out to Fort Hills, always inventing some excuse at the last moment. Instead, he kept luring me back, which wasn't hard to do. I was drawn by the daily crises, by the anarchy in the air and the smell of pain in the rooms of the old neighborhood, by the strange language and the angry words and the incomprehending looks and the close, smothering smells of cabbage and smoke and carpeted stairs and unhealthy desires that flourished under the flickering fluorescent coils of late night kitchens, where someone was always in trouble, and the quiet presence of death in the corners heightened life. There the ubiquitous cloud of the past helped me, finally, to see days of sun.

9

As it happened, the same week Hattie the wolf-girl left for college (a journey she deferred for a year while she worked to save some money), Paul enlisted in the army and took a bus to Georgia for basic training. On the ride down, he began worrying. Sitting beside a kid from Richdale who talked the whole way about the coming race war, he wondered if he'd ever see his family again. He thought of Hattie's betrayal, and felt the stirrings of forgiveness. After the war, when she finished college, if he made it, they could try again.

He was less indulgent toward Ada. For the last few years they had battled daily: he resented her efforts to control him; moreover, half-consciously he blamed her for his father's departure. He wondered if she might not be glad he was leaving—because he reminded her of Lev. He sucked his cigarette and closed his eyes, wishing he could turn down the volume on the manic mouth next to him.

Meanwhile, Adriana sat alone in her bedroom, weeping, while Nina and the other dead looked on.

"You wanna die or something?" Alex had said when Paul told him.

Vietnam looked like a bad scene, no matter what Nixon, who was a good guy, said. Watching some of the convention in Chicago, he felt exhilarated by the sight of kids only slightly older than him taking part in a world that most of the time seemed impossibly distant and closed. He didn't know what to make of hippies but he instinctively mistrusted the cops, who reminded him of his father.

"Good for me," Paul had shrugged. "Teach me something 'sides Johnson rods. I'm nineteen, for Crissakes!"

Alex didn't know what else to say: *Christ came down from the cross*, he read in a poem, wishing there was someone he could talk to, but the closest he came to finding a mentor was his art teacher, who in his conversations never ventured beyond art, and while this helped bring Alex out of himself, he longed for more practical guidance.

10

The envelope was postmarked Seattle. Ada had left it on his dresser where he found it when he came home from school. All mail from Vietnam was routed through Seattle.

Alex didn't open it right away. He had never received a letter before, only notes from girls at school.

These days, Alex was busy—his art teacher had urged him to enter a contest and he was up all hours working on a watercolor of a house with wings. He walked through the neighborhood with a sketch pad. How different things appeared when you slowed down. He saw the textures of brick in the pattern of light and shadows. When you just looked at things, they stared back. He studied rows of shoes in Kolber Sladkus and the mannequins in the window of Gimbels and the mausoleum of City Hall. It was April, and the long days kept him out late. He had had several phone conversations with Hattie, who'd gone away to school. She wasn't happy out in Indiana, and she asked about Paul but seemed just as interested in him.

Finally, one evening, he opened Paul's envelope. He was sitting alone on the stoop, smoking a cigarette. Though it was only a few sentences, the scrawl covered the better part of the page:

> Dear Alex,
>
> It is hot here. You have never been this hot unless you been places I don't know. Mosquitoes are the size of birds. The gooks are everywhere, and soon it's crazy eddie time, you know? Can you believe I miss Roosevelt? If I die, tell Hattie I love her. If I live, don't say a word. And mom too. Just kidding.

The individual letters were large and childlike. Since his brother's departure Alex had fallen in with a crowd that opposed the war, and he felt uncomfortable thinking of Paul running through a jungle carrying a gun. Until now Vietnam had seemed unreal, occupying the same imaginative territory as *Gilligan's Island* or *Star Trek*, something seen on the small screen that incited more of a response than other shows, certainly, but which, because it could be switched on and off, nevertheless belonged in the same category of experiences. Paul's note complicated matters.

When he returned on leave the first week of November, Adriana laid out a meal. In the months since his departure, she'd worried she'd driven her son away and she prayed to the Virgin Mary every night to keep him safe. She wanted to please him now, so she stayed up until after midnight, kneading dough, mashing potatoes, boiling pirohy, and cutting beets for borscht, as though she were making a Christmas Eve dinner. She covered the table with a white cloth and set out the dishes and silverware. It was nearly one in the morning by the time she finished her preparations. She poured herself a glass of wine and went over to the window where she looked down at the empty street under the full moon and remembered herself ice-skating across a pond.

Her efforts to connect with her son didn't work. Paul's reticence had deepened. On the surface he seemed more polite, as though tamed by the asparagus-green uniform Ada could not take her eyes off of, her reaction doubled-edged. Uniforms intimidated her and throughout the meal she kept dragging on her cigarette, sensing under his politeness a spirit gripped by anger, and it reminded her of her own experiences during the war. In a way, this was worse because back then neither she nor the others around her had been on the attack. Here, fear and confusion were compounded by guilt.

"Did they shoot at you?" she asked. Should she talk about it? He didn't seem to want to. And how could he answer? Did she really want to know?

He shrugged. The borscht bloodied his lips. His skin was tanned and suddenly he reminded Ada of the actor Victor Mature.

Her brother Viktor, who'd grown even more introverted, stared at his vodka as though it were a crystal ball. They all smoked throughout the meal: four cigarettes tipped in the trough of the ashtray.

Alex couldn't keep silent and when Paul tried to say something, Alex called him a fascist. "You're all fucking Nazis," he spat.

He expected his brother to get physical and felt betrayed when, instead of lashing out, Paul shook his head and his face trembled as though he were fighting back tears. He'd never seen his brother cry, not after their father left or when Hattie broke up with him, and he didn't think him capable of it, but he couldn't change how he saw things.

In the silence, with only the radiator clanking in the background, Alex became even more aggressive. He stared at his brother, challenging him.

To his surprise, Paul refused to argue. "You don't get it," was all he said.

Adriana sliced up the lindzer torte with an ominous-looking carving knife and they ate the rest of the meal in silence.

After dinner, Alex said he was feeling sick and excused himself. Alone in his room, he plugged his earphones into his AM/FM, tuning into the drugged-out sound of WBAI, the slur of debased melody evoking a funky world of pale, slow-moving skinny girls in stained silk underwear, bloods with Afros like the blown-up foil on a Jiffy Pop, and shirtless men in boxers with needle marks along their inner thighs. Here was adventure, luring him from his ghetto, this charmless neighborhood bristling with frustrated longings. Pietro, Sammy Cochon, Viktor the Spinner. He wanted to leave; he would leave. He was feverish, his naked flesh soaked the sheets. He wished he understood his brother. He dreamed he was in Vietnam and people were shooting at him because he'd cut off somebody's head while a palm tree sang a song by Billie Holiday. Toward morning, the fever subsided and he felt his energy return.

Over the next days, Paul didn't force conversation. He hung around Alex's room, smoking Camels. Paul was changed: he had the dark energy of a man tapped into his own psychotic spaces. His cropped hair made him look like a convict, and yet clearly he wanted to connect. He had something to tell him, Alex could feel it. Since Paul's departure, the house had felt too claustrophobic and now it was all edges and angles everywhere you turned.

Sometimes he called me in the evening to talk. We must have spent as much time on the phone as two teenage girls.

On Saturday Paul asked Alex to drive down with him to the shore.

On the ride down, in a car borrowed from a friend of Paul's, the brothers were silent except when they stopped for coffee. They sat at a table across from four cheerleaders in uniform and Paul leaned forward and said loudly: "Keep your eyes open and you'll catch some gap."

Twenty miles of silence followed.

As they turned off the highway, a truck pulled out in front of them and Paul had to swerve nearly off the road to avoid it.

The abrupt move triggered something in him and he began talking maniacally:

"You can't help it it's the nature of the system you're stuck with it you can lock the door but somebody will kick it down even if you're hiding or the house is burning because basically there are always at least two of you and you're fighting your fascist impulses all the time they're blasting you."

"You bet," Alex said not wanting to contradict him.

They drove through wetlands, glistening in the cool light, and Alex thought at that moment it would be fine to be an egret swimming in open air, so he leaped into the bird and cruised the sky for several miles.

"Sorry," Paul said.

Noon was bright, but gathering clouds and sea flakes salted the air they sprinted through down the boardwalk where they stopped before checking into the hotel. Paul pointed out Convention Hall where he'd gone with the track team years earlier as wind bossed gulls along the moody sky. One of the birds broke from the flock and landed on the railing where his cawing turned into a keen while beside them rose an atoll of lost sneakers—somewhere a team of semi-shod athletes must have been limping like a secret society.

They leapt off the boardwalk for the beach where Paul picked up a scallop shell and with a comic flourish handed it to his younger brother.

"Here's something from the oldest country of all."

The hotel had gingerbread, a wraparound porch, and was crowded with white wicker, though a few of the windows in the tower were boarded up. It was Alex's first night in a hotel and he had a feeling of giddy ceremony crossing the threshold. Their lime-colored room had two windows, one overlooking an airshaft, the other a side street. The bed was covered in beige chenille. Paul made them frisk it for fleas.

He came out of the shower naked and said to Alex, who lay on the bed watching television:

"You still a virgin?"

Alex ignored him. He poured them two fingers of Johnny Walker. *Forbidden Planet* was the feature on Channel 9's *Chiller Theater.* Suddenly he felt very happy to have his brother back and grateful for this adventure. It had been years since they'd gone anywhere together.

"Turn that off and let's go out. Grab the bottle," Paul said.

Downstairs, near the revolving door in the lobby, an old man shouted at a much younger woman with streaked blond hair, threatening her with a cigar, and a little boy crawled across the floor on his stomach in pursuit of a turtle.

They sat in dirty blue chairs under the half-blind chandelier, sucking the wick. Paul, who still had his sunglasses on, said the most useful thing he'd learned in the military was how to hammer a roach with a handgun. He'd show him later. The system, man, system is driving us nuts. Don't get sucked in.

After a spate of listless sentences, they walked to the rides where they went up in the roller coaster, as they had before on Coney Island. Later, they sat at the edge of the boardwalk, embracing the posts and listening to wind riding the water. Before heading to bed, Paul yanked off a sneaker and hurled it at the sea.

They returned home late the following afternoon, racing up the parkway under a slate sky. As they pulled up their street they saw Pietro on the corner, the crucifix on his back.

Ada had already left for work. Alex's head ached; he'd never been so hung over, so he took a hit off the joint Paul offered, then he stumbled into his room where he passed out. He dreamed about a wolf. He was the wolf and he was the hunters in red checks stalking it. As it crouched, preparing to leap for his throat, he shot it and woke to find that Paul had found his pistol, and Adriana was screaming. Dazed, he walked into the living room where he saw his brother's body pumping blood on the floor.

The funeral was a hazy affair, as though everyone attending were hung over, which, quite possibly, we were. A few of Paul's friends from school and the garage stood in the back of the church, and later I watched them slipping off to the bar before heading out to the cemetery.

Alex and I talked about Paul while walking along the railroad tracks. Only a couple of years had passed since the days when we imagined escaping to the Keys via Newport News, but so much had changed. Now that I no longer lived in the neighborhood, Alex appeared acutely sensitive to the differences in our circumstances, and while he never said anything about my parents, he spoke about his situation in a way that made it clear we were no longer on the same team facing the same hurdles. He was starting to feel cornered, I could see it; and that feeling, once it arrives, is hard to beat back. You can beat it back, but it keeps returning.

After describing their trip to Atlantic City, he said:

"Paul had to get away from Ada," he explained. "So do I. She wants something we can't give her."

"What's that?"

"I'm not sure."

He had his mother's eyes, his father's nose, his own wirey delicacy. His bronze hair hung down to his shoulders. He wore a turtleneck, a suede jacket, and a sailor's cap in imitation of the poet Ferlinghetti, whose book he'd found in a used bookstore on Liberty Street and which he bought for the title, *A Coney Island of the Mind*, because he'd been there. Alex also loved *Catcher in the Rye* and sometimes he talked about phonies, though I suspect he found Holden too innocent to believe. His boyhood eccentricities and compulsions had been reconfigured in ways that at the time appeared attractive: Alex had so much more direct experience of the world's harshness and therefore, it seemed, of reality itself, than I. I was sure he'd slept with a girl, though he never mentioned anyone. Despite all he'd seen and whatever he might have felt toward Ada, he seemed sure only a girl could save him.

At the same time, some things got to me. While he could be funny and playful, his ragging on society often took a hectoring turn, as though he had privileged insight and knew better than the rest of us what was wrong with the world. He could be too sure about things. Viktor had taught him a taste for booze, and when drunk he was capable of rages and fits, as Paul had been, and few experiences pleasure less than lectures delivered by a drunk.

Alex was growing into a working-class bohemian, becoming part of a small but identifiable clique whose members struggle to cultivate sensibilities in environments where fat fists and jeering mouths still rule. At sixteen, he'd already been working for a year in the storeroom of a local supermarket; my own father would not allow me to get a job. Yet he pursued his drawing and reading with more ardor than I ever felt for anything, and while he hadn't won the contest his teacher had urged him to enter, he felt sufficiently confirmed in his talent to speak of himself as an artist. Art was far from the lives of most of the émigrés and the working people of Roosevelt and merely proclaiming such a thing both alienated him from his immediate world and endowed him with a sheltering aura others respected.

Adriana now longed for her friends on the other side. She quit one diner, was fired from another for confusing her orders. Sometimes she called Mother late at night. She never complained, Mother said; instead she rambled on about the old country, remembering in detail games the girls had played, and the streets where they'd played them. While she listened to her old friend patiently, Mother refused to let herself be drawn more deeply into Ada's life.

For several weeks between jobs, Ada found herself at home with her brother, who drank and watched television all day. She began to shut the world out. The Kruks' apartment became a fortress of loneliness as each member of the household sank deeper into private revery. Eventually Ada's withdrawal was so complete, Alex said, that the mirrors took umbrage and refused to reflect her.

He noticed this when he walked into the bedroom to tell his mother he was leaving home. She curled on the double bed, from which she hadn't risen in days, her eyes unmarked, her lips pale.

"Mother," the young man with the shoulder-length hair said, "I'm leaving soon."

She lay, barely breathing, blank eyes open on the ceiling.

On his way out, he glanced into the mirror and saw that, according to it, the bed was empty.

"Mother, get up and eat something."

She didn't move. What should he do?

"Mother, stop it."

He wanted to leave—knew that if he didn't he'd wind up like Paul.

She wanted him to stay.

"Leave me alone," she said.

Frightened, Alex slipped out and found Uncle Viktor, who sat in his room watching an old black and white television.

"Drink?" Viktor asked.

"Sure," Alex said.

Viktor poured him a glass of vodka and listened. As Alex spoke, Viktor stood up and began spinning. He spun around and around and Alex grew dizzy watching him, his anger dissolved in confusion.

11

Late one Saturday morning, April of my junior year, I caught a ride to Roosevelt from Father, who was visiting a former patient.

I dropped by the Kruks' unannounced.

Adriana opened the door, cigarette in hand. Her head was tilted back slightly, the better to take in the show. Black rings rimmed her eyes like circles drawn by an excited student taking a test.

Seeing me, she smiled.

"He's not here," Ada said. "But you come in."

She sat me down on a stiff chair in the living room. All the curtains were drawn. I could hear Viktor coughing in the next room. The apartment reeked of old smoke. That was the first time I saw the wallpaper with the hunting scenes hung in honor of Anton.

Gazing at her, I barely recognized the beauty I'd leaped up to kiss only five years earlier. Yet her presence saturated the room. The curtains shivered with her and the chair stood on tiptoe, eager to please. Though she had not yet said a word, her eyes—so much like Alex's—began to shine, as though she'd heard my thoughts.

"You remind me of Anton," she said. Wine on her breath.

"The poet?"

It was as though both of us had erased the disasterous performance from our memory banks.

I shrugged. Looking like a poet didn't appeal to me. A rock star, or maybe an astronaut.

"Your mother must be proud of you," she said, apropos of nothing.

Confused, I looked away.

"Alex is a good artist," I said, breaking the silence waiting inside the green wallpaper to swallow us again.

She stared at me as though I were an experiment that was giving her a little trouble.

"They used to call me the giraffe," she said, laughing softly.

She reached her hand out and stroked my bristles. Father had taken me to a barber for a crew cut. I suddenly wanted hair long as Alex's. Feeling Ada's hand on the hateful stubble made me shiver.

Viktor coughed again. In the apartment below, someone turned up *La Traviata* (Mother was a buff, always borrowing records from the library and I often listened along with her).

"You're like a poet," she repeated, lids lowered, eyes aflame. The air felt humid and I sensed a prickling through my chest and arms. She put out her cigarette.

Ada's face was very near mine. I could almost smell the grease and smoke from the diner through the soap.

She took my hand, stroked my fingers, put them on her forehead, then on her nose, touching it to her lips, her chin. Finally she rested my hand on her breast, and both of us made a little noise.

She put my hand on her breast.

It lasted only a few hours—whatever that means: time is elastic and can be measured neither in minutes, nor in grains of sand, nor by the waters of the clepsydra. In a way, it never ended.

We felt that heightened awareness which accompanies the crossing of any closed border. We knew that everything we saw and did would be forever changed, and that must have been what we wanted: a different world, a world transformed.

She put my hand on her breast. She wore a blue cotton dress, simple as the sky. Either my hand or her breast was damp—I remember the moisture and slight stickiness as fabric bunched around her nipple. This was not my first breast. That had belonged to Dolores Garcia, who'd let me claim a bit of it in her attic the previous month. But this was so much larger and grander, it was another thing entirely. Her green eyes locked mine in the guardrail of their gaze. Strange things happened: they opened suddenly and I sank through them like a chutist in free fall. All her reserve collapsed. I kept going.

Soon her dress was off and I was staring at the freckled, doe-colored skin of a forty-year-old woman. Maybe the flesh sagged and folded over itself, but it was no less than a sighting of Atlantis, a place out of time. The rest of our clothes dissolved as though they were spun of sugar. She was a garden enclosed: an orchard of pomegranates, with pleasant fruits; camphire, with spikenard. Spikenard and saffron; calamus and cinnamon, with trees of frankincense; a well of living waters, and streams from Lebanon. So I gathered the myrrh and ate the honeycomb with my milk.

She kissed my eyelids and stroked my hair tenderly as a cat licking afterbirth off her newborn.

The press of flesh to flesh, tongue to tongue, left me reeling. What mattered more was that while we lay beside each other, she understood exactly what I was thinking, and I knew her mind as though it were my own. I discovered how love enlarges intelligence, how it lights all things, and that nothing that comes before it remains dark. It was a great lesson.

Afterwards, though, nothing was ever said: I just found excuses each time Alex called. Homework. Basketball. My newfound girlfriend. Soon it wasn't just the business with Ada. I wanted Roosevelt behind me. The old worlds, all of them, felt tired.

Did Alex suffer my absence? Did he feel I'd betrayed him? Did he know how I had?

That evening, on the ride to Port Authority in New York, where I went to catch a bus back to Fort Hills, I kept replaying the afternoon, pouring over it with memory's magnifying glass. Her breasts, her belly, her knees. Tan stockings on the dark-stained dresser. Naked flesh in the mirror. The filtered sunlight freckled with motes. Snippets of images swarming like moths. I grew excited and had to shield myself with my hands. Not that the wheezing drunk next to me would have noticed. I kept thinking about our last hour together. The bedroom. The dark red carpet. And what she told me in between, after the first time. She began with flashes of the sea, her parents, a monastery in the Crimea, the gypsy. Later she gave me Anton's story to read and I wondered how much of what she told me had been memory and how much imagination. Her eyes read the ceiling and her voice was small, as though she didn't want to witness what she herself was about to say. She rambled on about the war, visiting her aunt's, ice-skating on the snow-covered pond. Then she told me about the soldier who raped her. I drank in this moment of horrific life, my heart pounding, a strange cruel excitement surging inside me.

"Silly. So long ago," she finished. Then she turned over on her belly and wiped the sweat that had bubbled up over my face and arms with her tongue.

"How old are you? Fifteen?"

I said nothing, hoping by silence to add a few years to my evident ignorance.

She sat with the quilt under her heavy breasts and talked. She loved to talk, she said, but no one was around to listen. Her loneliness was the emergency we were tending. She told me about her father and mother. She remembered her brothers and sisters, some of whom were still alive, though she hadn't heard from them in years. She even explained Nina.

Alex didn't come back that afternoon. If Viktor emerged, I never saw him. When we were done—and I was done quickly, twice—Adriana dressed in silence while I watched from the bed, the covers gathered under my chin, too bewildered to move. Then she turned to me and spoke. Her voice was stern and full of authority. Paternal more than maternal. It sounded odd, considering that minutes ago our mouths had mapped a new country.

"Listen, Nicholas: you'll never come here again. Sometimes, doors open. Secret doors. Doors nobody else knows about.

Nobody must ever know. No one will ever know. What happened is unrepeatable. You have it in your memory forever. Enjoy it," she smiled. Playful, but also, I think, a little cruel.

I said nothing. Sweat broke out again over my forehead. I touched her cracked lips, whose color had erased itself over my body, saying nothing. My heart pounded.

Later, she watched me dress as intently as I had stared at her—as though she were saying good-bye to something with her eyes. Not just me; something larger.

I would glimpse her now and then when we came to Roosevelt for holidays. After Mass I'd talk to Alex outside, and we'd make plans that we never followed up. And I didn't speak to Adriana again until after my parents' death.

Of course, that was not it. Our midday duet became a set-piece in my fantasy life for months. Years. I believed I was in love with her. My heart ached. Yet I wouldn't disobey her. She told me to stay away, and I did. Eventually, the images grew frayed, and when Dolores Garcia came more sharply into focus, they faded sufficiently for me to pursue more appropriate adventures.

But the stories Ada let slip kept curling back into my mind like fragments of my own dream. They seemed so unlikely they had to be real, and I have never lost the need to put them together in a way that makes a firmament of history out of which might emerge in the future a fate less tragic than that of Ada and her sons.

The Woman Who Defeated Stalin

1

I went to college in Boston. Not long after I arrived I had a call from Alex, who said he was moving north himself.

The Kruko hadn't applied to schools. He aspired to paint but was the first to admit he lacked discipline, and Ada was too distracted to direct him. Going where I lived gave him a touchstone.

I told him to phone me again after he arrived; when he did, I was too busy to see him.

He put behind him Roosevelt, Viktor, his mother and her religious manias. He took a room at the YMCA on Huntington Avenue where he lived for a month. At night he lay in bed watching his desires scatter across the ceiling like insects. This was his only time on earth and it unfolded with a fury he couldn't control. What could he do but give in? Which he did, for years, while Ada pursued him with letters he carried weeks before opening.

Wanting some sort of affiliation, he joined the Institute for Imaginative Living, a group home operated by a man named Serge. It was based in an old Queen Anne in Somerville, until recently a working-class city, mainly Italian and Irish, streaked with Haitian—one might call it cosmopolitan, if that didn't suggest a glamour the place never had. Imagine Paris without lights, without art, without original or interesting architecture. Triple deckers, thickets of antennae, rooms decorated with sea shells. Houses like shipwrecks and islands of lost souls. There are no pockets of flamboyant wealth in Somerville: no Brattle Streets, Rue Vaugirards, Fifth Avenues, or Via Venetos. In the forties, it was the third most densely populated city in the world. Each house is flanked on either side by a gas station or a muffler repair shop and everywhere there are garages, car wash palaces, auto parts emporiums. Mild madonnas in blue gowns grace the yards of the older residents, and Christmas lights, tacked to the shingles, on night and day, suggest Candyland. The natives toil in garages and local factories, stuffing pillows, stocking food on grocery shelves, selling papers, typing letters, serving in greasy spoons, and scraping pasta dishes—Alex saw his mother everywhere. They were good people, passably thrifty (though belonging to a debtor nation); industrious (though finding room in the day for seven hours of television); and generally good. They even liked what they did.

For that, Serge hated them. It was on their backs the middle classes rose. They let themselves be the coal and the oil in the roaring furnaces of the rich. Serge wanted them to be the dynamite. He'd composed a mission statement, which he'd mimeographed and posted in laundromats and on telephone poles around town:

> We at the Institute know that life's major lessons are learned outside the classroom. We have found a way to teach you the

> things they don't teach you in school. Our students study betrayal, blackmail, beating, fraud, incest, lying, sexism, and stealing, all in a structured environment. We teach ambition, greed, lust, jealousy, and rage, driving people to these states so that they can later learn to control them. There are reasons why we Americans need such an education now as never before in our history. The war that taught the young so much is ending, while semi-clandestine experiences don't seep out into the larger population, leaving only an elite with insight into what humans are capable of. We at the Institute are committed to tearing down the curtain on human nature.

Alex was thrilled to find others who saw the world as he did. I suggested it was flaky, but he accepted their absurdities. Accepted may be too strong. He needed a structure that would help this survivor of the disappearing sickness from being flattened by a world that loomed over him like a glacier preparing to crush a lone skiff in a squall. It's likely Ada's obsessive retailing of stories about their social standing in the old world infuriated him, and he responded by sidling up to an American version of the very politics that had destroyed his parents' families. As Ada turned increasingly inward, to an idealized past, her son stalked a utopian future.

Several months passed before I was able to see him. Finally, at Alex's invitation, I attended a meeting at the Institute.

It was just after Thanksgiving; the season's first snow had fallen that morning and I borrowed a scarf from my roommate before going out.

He met me at the door of the old Victorian house. In the city, Alex's bohemianism took a flamboyant turn: the gloves and turtleneck were replaced by a fringed jacket and cowboy boots with red tooling. The effect of his costumes, however, was tempered by the fact that so many of our civilian peers donned uniforms, as though competing with the military. His thin black hair was long, but the rest of his face was closely shaved, angular, permanently pale; he looked about sixteen. He threw his arms around me in a manly hug. He was so glad to see me, I regretted not calling earlier.

Inside, we listened to Serge deliver a sermon about science. We sat in a circle in a dark living room surrounded by portraits of Mao, Lenin, and Che while a wiry man with a narrow face and large ears held forth. The species was mutating, he said. I couldn't help staring at his ears, which reminded me of catcher's mitts. To what might they have been an adaptation?

The disruptions of the first half of the century, Serge continued, the wars, followed by the upheavals of the sixties and early seventies, commanded us to change—be a part or stand apart, the slogan of the future. Something new had begun. Society was evolving. Serge encouraged the citizens, as he called his devotees, to develop an enemies list. "Why should the president be the only one?"

Then he went on to attack the recent antinuclear rally in Central Park:

"Fucking preppy environmentalists. They can deal with Mother Earth. With seals and owls. But they won't see you if you're poor. Believe me, they hire from their own class. If they give you a break and let you in, they'll always be watching for proof of what you can't do. They need to think it's merit, see, that makes their money. Merit, not privilege."

Five or six other people scattered in chairs around the room seemed to range in age from sixteen to well into their fifties. They faced their leader attentively, sniffling and nodding, while a calico cat dozed on the window sill.

The radiator spat as I unspooled the scarf and wrapped it around my fist under the gaze of old and new revolutionaries.

A steamless discussion followed the talk, after which Alex and I walked through snow to the Plough, an Irish pub near the printing shop where Alex had found work.

The well-lit bar was crowded and elbows jostled our ribs while a moist smoke sagged in blown bales from the ceiling. The air was sour with beer. Everybody in the place was Irish, including the women—blonds, redheads, brunettes. In school I was touched by the pride of the Irish: even the jocks persuaded you they were fluent in the work of Yeats and Joyce. Galway fiddlers rocked the juke and Guinness glistened in our mugs. Outside, the Charles River flowered into the Liffey. Being Irish seemed fabulous and comprehensive and it left me feeling isolated and Ukrainian.

"You buy that shit?" I asked about Serge, pint in hand.

Alex shrugged.

"Whatever's going on, I have no way into it, gumba. You can fight but you know it'll never happen. They're too strong. *Christ climbed down.*"

"What about school?"

"Who's gonna pay?"

I said there were scholarships and offered to help, but we were eighteen and all decisions were provisional and subject to daily revision: no vows yet because life was a kingfisher, diving into the stream, soaring up with something flopping in its mouth. Mysteries teemed. Around us, the crowd reeled.

"Listen, Nick, I'll figure it out. I have ideas. I'll paint, get a gallery. Use the bucks from sales to buy a supply store. Maybe host a radio show at night."

"Great."

The city had stirred him with a sense of how much could be done. Suddenly he had ambitions.

He ran his fingers through his long hair and tossed his head back nervously.

"Weather persecutes the poor," he laughed. "Ever notice? Trailer parks are the first to go in a tornado."

I asked about home.

He scratched his ear.

"I'm outta there. I love Ada, but she was killing me. Know?"

"Should be on your own," I agreed, wondering what I'd have done without the structure of school. "How's the painting?"

"Great. Ever hear of Goya?"

I nodded, lying.

"He's the man. All that war. Check it out."

"Sure."

We drank our pints.

"Hear about Ai?" he asked after a while.

Ai was one of the Florentina girls—Hattie's sister.

"Baby. Moved back home. Hattie too."

"Kidding."

"All coming back. Can't escape it, bro. Except you."

"And you," I replied, and he winked.

"Check her," he said, tipping his head toward a blond near the door.

He wanted to play, as though we were still kids in the Catskills.

Soon Alex was wired into a world of excitements I didn't find on campus, where occasional marches gave respite from theory. In school, I kept to myself; with Alex, I cut loose.

Alex was driven. Freed of maternal restraints, he found the world promising resolutions to appetite. He wasn't handsome, but he trembled with an energy he barely contained, which emanated from him like shining from shook foil. He'd arrived in a place where everything was rootless and weightless, making it easy to drift from one woman to another. Or to a mother? Was that it? None of his girls ever came into focus. They were like water in which he kept finding his own puckered face.

Sometimes, drunk, he said strange things, claimed objects communicated with him, knives asked him to use them, beds begged to be slept in, clothes refused to be worn. Yet he'd always been fanciful, a victim of the disappearing sickness, a lover of free verse, and I discounted the weirdness.

One night at the Plough I found him in a dark mood. He barely looked at me, staring instead at the floor, hiding under his cowboy hat.

It must have been the weekend because the bar was bursting. After downing a few shots, he reached into the pocket of his fringed jacket and pulled out a sheet of thin blue paper, which he thrust at me. I hunched down, rocked by the crowd, half-drunk myself, and in dim light read:

> Dear Alex,
>
> I am sure you very busy with work. Viktor and I survive, thank you Jesus. Beatrice takes me to mall where Hattie

works. Remember, we are one soul. This is mystery. I wish you visit but I know you are work hard. Don't forget you prayers. The most important in life.

Yesterday the phone call told me your father died last week.

Despite the broken grammar, the handwriting was neat. I was surprised she wrote him in English but supposed it was her way of reaching out.

I put my hand on his shoulder. He shrugged it off.

"Fucker."

He ordered another round, then glanced to me to pay for it.

"Glory to the motherland, brother," he said.

From the juke, a strain of violins like sweaty horses surging homeward rocked the room. The guy in a blue jersey next to Alex must have knocked his elbow because his pint glass shattered on the floor. My friend wheeled round and spat:

"Fucking mick bastard."

It was Warinenco Park all over. This time, without Officer Mike. My six inches on Alex was overshadowed by the short-haired bull in blue who gaped at us, bewildered.

Before I could grab him, Alex had jumped the jostler, roping his neck with his own thin arms.

The rodeo lasted seconds and ended with Alex on the floor and both of us out the door while a snorting beefy herd jeered directives, telling us where to go. His hat was left hostage.

I dragged Alex up through the slush. The street lamps on that block had gone out and the bright moon's veins were clearly visible. Alex's nose was bleeding and a tooth had loosened. Once out of sight of the bar, we stopped, and he scooped up some snow and buried his face in it while I stood beside him, looking anxiously down the street.

Soon after getting that letter about his father, he finally went back to visit Ada, a trip he later described to me in painful detail.

She appeared at the door in a red robe. She blinked, seeing him there, as though she wasn't quite sure who he was. She looked down and adjusted her glasses. Suddenly she was older. Her hair was wrapped in a babushka, a style he hadn't see before. Her lipstick was smudged as though she'd been sleeping.

He stopped at the threshold and sniffed the air like a hound.

The apartment smelled of fried food and cigarettes.

"Come eat," she said after a few seconds.

"I'm not hungry."

He walked in.

"Where's Viktor?"

"I'll just put a few things on the table," she said, turning toward the kitchen while Alex walked on down the hall. He hadn't heard the mother tongue in a while.

He pushed open the door to his old room. He and his brother had grown up here. The closet still bulged with their clothes.

From the wall opposite the bed depended a three-foot silk screen of his father's face that he'd done from a photograph. The stern, thick-browed eyes were neutralized by the comic-book colors Alex had used: Day-Glo pinks and tangerines. It reminded him of the posters at the Institute. There was a connection between family pictures and the posters of dictators, he'd concluded, fighting to reach the bottom of his breath.

He searched his pocket for a bottle of Valium he'd persuaded a doctor to prescribe.

Across the hall was Viktor's room. Former site of the Museum of the Horrors of History. Now a large wooden cross hung above the single bed covered in a beige chenille quilt. Against the opposite wall stood a desk and bookshelves on cinder blocks crammed with volumes in several languages alongside half a row of black marbled notebooks in which Viktor wrote journal entries, poems, stories. Evenings, while he and Paul had watched television, Viktor had sat in a chair, drink in hand, scribbling. When Alex asked what, Viktor had replied, "My memoirs, dear child."

Alex took one off the shelf and slowly opened to a random page. His eye alighted on an epigraph from Pascal: *And the sole aim of scripture is charity*. He closed the book and put it back on the shelf.

After flicking the light switch in the hall, he went and sat down in the dining room where Ada had already laid out the formal placemats, the good china, even silverware. On every wall hung either a cross or a picture of Jesus.

"Why did you turn on the light?"

She looked at him over the rose-colored frames.

"It's dark, Mother."

She shook her head, sitting down.

The room was warm as though an oven door had been left open.

"I was fifteen when my mother died," she began, placing the bowl before him.

A light chicken broth with noodles. Alex ladled himself a second helping.

"They arrested people whenever they wanted. Sometimes they shot them in the street. They liquidated the ghetto. You know what that means. We lived across from the police station. Sometimes I would go out in the morning for school and have to step over a body on the sidewalk.

"I don't even know the names of the people who killed my father. I feel very close to them. I think about them every night."

He couldn't understand the clawing at his heart, this pain in his chest, a great panic veering without warning to rage that he choked down. His mother, for Christ's sake. Why did seeing her leave him with sweaty palms and dark impulses?

"I don't remember much about Mother's parents. We visited their farm, the largest in the village. Your great-grandfather bred roses. He could write. He thought Tolstoy an idiot. He argued with Mother, who loved the Russian. But Mother didn't talk much. And when she opened her mouth, it was usually to tell you how wrong you were.

"Do you want some pie? Apple. Hot."

"Later."

"Will you stay? I'll make the room."

She wanted him to stay as much as he needed to go.

When he shook his head, her face dropped. She pushed herself from the table and began shouting, her voice rising higher until he imagined her transfigured into a screeching crane:

"You! I look at you but I don't see anybody there. I'm sorry to tell you. I made you and you're nothing. How can you forget your mother like this? Don't you know why people have children? We dragged you here for a reason. Translators. We needed translators. Blind, unnatural child. Devil has you. Go to him. Him and your whores."

She stopped. Her hands went up to her scarf and she plucked it off, spilling a sheaf of silvery gold hair that hung limply around her still strong face.

In a calm voice, she said:

"Father Myron scared me with his talk about the Sermon on the Mount yesterday. I saw him slip out of his little body and rise to a place high above us. *Woe unto you that are full,* he said, *for ye shall hunger*. I was full at the time and I looked at the other women in the parish and they were all equally full. They'd been hungry once. We'd all been hungry once and we couldn't forget that. I felt the flesh on my hips and my breasts. Corns, veins, sore knees: these hold me here, keep me from reaching higher. I was hungry and now I'm full, which means one day I'll be hungry again."

She sounded like a girl, pleading for comfort he was unable to offer. He watched resentment flood her face.

"Why do you listen?" she asked.

"What?"

"You're here for the stories. Don't you have any of your own?"

"I do," he defended himself. "Plenty. I can't tell you."

"Why not?"

"They're not son-to-mother stories. That's all. Not even son-to-father stories. More like sinner-to-priest. But I don't know any priests."

"Oh come on."

She fell back in her chair, exhausted, and closed her eyes. He thought she was about to fall asleep. Her lids rose lazily, her eyes magnified by the glasses:

"I know why. Because they're better. My stories are better than yours."

She reached into her sweater and pulled out a cigarette, which she lit with a heavy silver lighter picked up from the table.

He let the insult settle before lashing back:

"Won't anything get through? We go over the same shit every time! I'm sick of it. I hate the old world."

"I know," she replied, smoke curling from her mouth. "And since you do, mind turning out the light when you go?"

On the Greyhound to Boston he sat in the back and smoked. He felt a sharp pain in his chest, a pulsing behind his eyes. He pressed two fingers to his lids but the tears came anyway. The pleasures he pursued did little to erase the grief he fled. He saw his mother's face as clearly as though she were sitting beside him, pasting green stamps into booklets, talking to Nina and her other brothers and sisters. The thought of these lost uncles, some alive, most dead, confused him. He remembered Paul's rap about the system, the system that lay behind everything. So many immigrants did well in America. Poster children for the new world. Outside headlights raced by in the dark. We're such loners here. He pulled a flask of peppermint schnapps from his pocket and took a swig. He remembered ice skating in the moonlight upheld by his parents, Paul in his red cap several feet ahead. What had happened to everyone?

Then he fell in love and I didn't see him for nearly six months. He called a few times and told me about her but we never met. All I know was that her name was Helen and that they worked together. What they did, where they went, remain mysteries. It was just as well because that year I decided to declare pre-med and I staggered under the coursework, which I enjoyed without loving it, content to pursue what seemed the family business, but wondering all the while at the detachment I felt, as though I were on a ship staring out at the sea through a portal.

Alex's relationship ended badly. He called one night to tell me she'd left him. Obviously drunk, he said he was back at the Institute—I hadn't realized he'd moved. Now we could resume our meetings.

I don't know when Alex began consorting with the criminal element, but one night he took me to a party in the company of an exotic dancer named Boots, together with two of her friends, a man I was told was a gangster and his girlfriend, also a dancer, to a house in Framingham that sprawled like a country inn run by Caligula. Jimi Hendrix, one of the recent honored dead, pounded from the speakers as though trying to shout his way back from the grave. There I saw sights I'd never imagined took place off screen. In the den, before a noisy fire, a woman played a private show for guests crammed into a red leather couch. Dancing before the walk-in fireplace, blazing despite the forsythia blooming outside, she peeled off her jeans, and her blue denim cowgirl shirt hung open.

In the kitchen I found Boots leaning against the wall, eyes closed, sucking a joint. She had a long jaw, slitty eyes. I asked for a toke and we began talking. I fell in love near the sink. Our courtship was brief; the honeymoon, urgent. The divorce was equally swift. I don't remember when or how I got home.

For a long time after that, I ignored Alex's calls. I couldn't keep up: his life was one long breaking of the vessel, an endless shattering of personality and self.

Drinking, drugs, women: in an age of excess, Alex was of his age, and eventually he paid for it.

Like Ada, he had trouble keeping a job. Work was subordinate to private life. Arguing with his bosses seemed second nature and arriving late his right. After a fight with Serge, he left the Institute and returned to the Y. Around the same time he began reading the mystics—Boehme, Eckhart, Weil—who enjoyed an unlikely vogue with the bohemian crowd.

One evening, the summer after my first year of medical school, he called and said he was in a hospital in Jamaica Plain, and the next day I took the Green Line out to visit him.

July heat fogged the windows. A jowly man with limp gray locks slumped against the wall, hoping the metal might cool him as we rattled past the Museum of Fine Arts where Dallin's Indian on horseback appealed to the Great Spirit. Only an elderly

Korean woman in a sleeveless green dress seemed unmoved by the heat and sat humming a show tune.

The outward, medicated calm of psychiatric wards: walking among patients who seemed so self-possessed made me want to belt out "Singing in the Rain" and punctuate it by throwing a chair through a window. The place reminded me of high school, with mattresses in place of desks, a bouquet of rubbing alcohol in the air.

He was sitting on his bed, poring over some color Xeroxes. His cheeks had puffed out and he'd grown a moustache.

"Looks good," I said, indicating the moustache.

I gestured at the papers in his lap.

"Goya. *Third of May.*"

He handed me a sheet: a man in a white shirt and mustard pants stood before a firing squad, arms raised in fear and invitation. Seven faceless executioners aimed long rifle barrels at his chest.

"Goya watched Napoleon's men shooting people right outside his window," Alex explained.

I nodded, handing back the page, wondering how he knew these things, from where he'd gathered bits of history and lore.

"I'm using them as models," he explained, offering another wad.

I flipped through the smeared sheets, pen and ink sketches of body parts.

"I'm calling it *The Russian Revolution*."

"Important to keep working," I said.

He nodded. Then he shrugged and gestured at the beige walls: "A clean, well-lighted et cetera at last," he said. "Smokes?"

I handed him the carton of Marlboros I'd picked up.

"Let's go public."

A woman in a hairnet and pink housecoat sat alone in the windowless waiting room. Seeing us, she frowned.

"Look, a tarantula sucking on Negro brains," she screamed, pointing at me.

"Hey, Sal," Alex replied softly.

She rose, brought both hands to her mouth and made like she was shredding something with her teeth. Then she stomped out.

"That's Sally. Sit," he pointed to an aqua vinyl chair. He seemed sedated, but not entirely flattened.

I asked him how he felt and he said he was glad for a break. When he got out, he planned to look for a new job and spend more time with his art.

He asked how I was; I told him about school. I recall I mentioned a girl, a tall, vital, black-haired woman who seemed to keep a protective distance from the rest of the class, and with whom I hadn't spoken yet. She was clearly gifted and it was obvious the professors loved her. I had no idea that I was talking about Shelley who, years later, became my wife.

"Admit it," he smiled. "You always knew I'd wind up here."

"You haven't wound up here."

"Right. It's a break. Said that myself."

His collapse began with a vision. He said he couldn't explain it, but what he saw changed him. Nothing was real; the world was an illusion. Millions knew this, it wasn't a secret.

There was no fanatical edge to his voice, though he didn't look at me but eyed some spot over my left shoulder.

"Can I just tell you? Do you mind? I don't care, but I have to tell someone."

"Sure."

"I saw a half-dressed woman through a window. A snake coming at me then being driven back—that's right, a snake," he repeated. "And a black man carrying a suitcase getting off a train station in the middle of nowhere. That's it."

"That's it?"

"That's all I saw. But then I came to this place inside me where everything was light. I mean explosions. Ecstasy, big time. And out of it I came back with three things: God is everywhere, but you can't know a thing about Him and anybody who claims to is lying; and, you know, the usual stuff about love. The rest? Politics. Just fucking politics."

He'd gotten excited.

"Shouldn't talk about it," he added.

"Why?"

"Nothing to say," he shrugged, suddenly flat, and I dropped the matter. Then:

"You believe in God?"

"I don't know," I said, wanting a cigarette.

"Read the mystics."

"What do they do for you?"

A voice in the next room cried: "Kill the fucking camels!"

"That's what was missing at the Institute."

There was more missing than that, I wanted to say, like common sense.

"Serge talked only politics. Like power relations were all that mattered."

He said these things as though we were discussing daily matters. Dostoevsky Junior.

Finally I asked:

"Have you talked to Ada, paesano?"

He dropped his eyes.

"You haven't told her."

"Nick, I haven't seen her in over a year. She writes me letters. Sometimes I don't even read them. When I go home I only get depressed. There's never been anything I could figure out to do for them, her and Viktor. Short of kids. I know she'd like that. Don't think I'm up to it, though," he forced a smile.

"Want me to call her?"

He thought this over a while. The late light filtered in through dusty plastic blinds. Outside the city was on fire. Inside the air-conditioned silence everything slowed. We were like food in a refrigerator, our natural decay retarded to a crawl.

"No," he finally shook his head. "I know, you think I'm tough on her."

"I've never said that."

"No idea. You have no idea what it was like. This is Club Med after Grove Street. I know you feel sorry for her. She gave you that stupid story of Anton's to read, didn't she? Gives it to everybody. Who knows what's true? I sure don't. You? Bunch of Nazis. You know all the stories. The whole damn Ukrainian mess. They fucked everybody, everybody fucked them, and now their stories fuck us."

Self-hatred in his eyes. I knew what he meant—the Ukrainian story was so tangled, it was hard to separate truth from myth, or to decide whose version to believe. Easier to forget it entirely.

Sal drifted back into the room.

I stood up.

"Call me," I said and walked down the hall toward the elevator, leaving him alone in the forest of attempted suicides and angry dreamers.

Alex could be out of the hospital in a week. After that, what would he do? How would he support himself? What kind of a life would he make?

I didn't take the time to wonder and he didn't bother staying in touch.

Years passed before I heard from him again. I remember it was just after I'd returned from a conference where I'd finally managed a date with Shelley, which turned out to be much more charged than I could ever have anticipated. Despite the complications, I was excited and felt myself seized by one of those periodic updrafts that carry you along, if you're willing.

Alex had had another breakdown. This time, he was in Vermont, on a private farm in Barnet, outside Saint Johnsbury, where I visited him one afternoon in late spring when the leaves were fresh on the trees.

I saw him from a distance, waiting for me by the porch of a large blue Victorian house. It was a brilliant day and the oaks seemed to stretch out and embrace the air.

Standing at the foot of the stairs, he looked smaller. His shoulders were hunched and he held his arms in front of him like a praying mantis. His face, once so animated, was thin and dense with worry. The moustache was gone. Yet as I came up to him, he broke into a smile, opened his arms and hugged me.

I swore to myself I wouldn't neglect him again.

It was an experimental program. Patients slept in suites where the glass had been removed from the windows so only the screens remained. Several dozen finches and parakeets were then uncaged and released into the room.

Alex lived in an aviary.

He invited me in. I stood beside him watching a squad of screeching rainbows tear the air.

He smoked cigarette after cigarette, his face shadowy and absorbed.

"They won't mind," he said.

I didn't ask who was paying for the treatment.

A finch perched on a lamp dove at the seeds on the coffee table. Another bathed in a cup in the sink.

"Old Caribbean remedy of Dr. Walcott's," he explained.

"Hard to sleep at first. Whenever one makes a noise, the whole flock flares like a wave of gas suddenly lit. Cool, though."

While the birds sang and fluttered about, we sat in the room for an hour and talked about the Black Pond. I didn't bring up Ada. He asked about Boston, and I updated him in on the progress of the presidential primaries.

After many silences, I finally stood up and hugged him again and told him he'd be fine and insisted he see me back in the city.

On my way out I stopped at the main desk and left him an envelope with some money. I was still a student and the amount was piddling.

Alex became the friend whose voice you're glad to hear until you remember why you lost touch in the first place. He called when my mother died but never made it to the funeral. I dropped him a card when I got married. He sent one back, congratulating us. About a year ago he phoned on a Sunday morning and we talked nearly an hour. I told him about Shelley, my work. He seemed pleased. He said he was living in a halfway house in Somerville and had a job washing dishes in a good restaurant. He didn't complain. It was his mother's life. We discussed Ada and he said he was trying to make friends with her but it was slow going: he'd visit, they'd fight—over the same things (old country, no children) and Viktor would sit smoking while the two screamed at each other, with desperate love.

We said we'd meet for coffee, but we never did.

2

My parents died within six months of each other—Mother of a heart attack, just as she was about to dab perfume at the Estee Lauder counter in Macy's; Father of a stroke soon after—though in truth I'd diagnose it termination by longing, the last act of a will that could enlist death itself into its program. Their disappearance devastated me. Nothing had prepared me for this sensation of walking the tightrope with no net below. I'd had none of the usual complaints to lay at their door. When my peers, including Alex, rose in rebellion, I sat on the sidelines, sympathetic to both but puzzled by the frenzy. My only charge against my parents was that they were a little absent. They were busy; I was busy; we were all far too busy. After a point, they gave me no deeper sense of the past. While my grandmother was still alive back in the old country it seemed important to them; once she died and they moved to Fort Hills and found themselves separated from the collective, their sense of communal identity weakened. She died before Father had established himself and her death left him wanting nothing so much as to close the door on the past.

By the time I was in high school, they seemed to have sprung full grown from the soil of their own imaginations, which, wherever they may have started, quickly became remarkably conventional and American. By then my mother had grown so large it was hard for her to squeeze into the front seat of the blue Oldsmobile.

My first twelve years I lived in a closed community which couldn't have been more different from that of my neighbors. While this estranged me from my peers, it also gave me purpose and definition that were altered by our move to the suburbs. There traditions were supplanted by instructions in a stream of increasingly complex practical skills enabling me to adapt with ease. Assimilation, however, is never straightforward or painless—to a degree, sanity and humanity depend on keeping faith with a self over time. Without access to your childhood, you risk slipping into the land of Ulro, as the poet Blake called that place where individuals meet each other at the level of appearances alone.

In any case, I surrendered to my immediate world, to work, to relationships—a word we use to neuter love, reducing it to a hobby—and, when I had the time, to sports. In the winter I ski; summers I hunker down in a fishing village outside Orono, Maine, where the flashing of the lighthouse throws shadows on my bedroom walls and where only the occasional presence of a Penobscot Indian at the general store reminds me that the surrounding reality is not a moving picture of eternity. For two weeks a year I sail in the mornings and play tennis in the afternoon. The efficiency of my well-oiled life assures me that each time I use my ATM card I participate in a ritual older than prayer, so effortlessly have the technological changes of the last decades integrated themselves.

And it is not enough.

From their funerals I retain a collage of snapshots. Both services were held at St. Bridget's, a bland modern building better suited to bingo than prayer, and were presided over by the pleasant Father Durgin, who'd never laid eyes on my father and who kept calling my mother Helen instead of Slava. As Father's coffin sank, I heard someone playing "Amazing Grace" on bagpipes at another service not ten headstones away.

On both days the weather was mild and sunny, which seemed a kind of generosity toward them, a gesture of respect, though the sun's brightness the afternoon we buried my father left me queasy and feverish. Father Durgin was gentle yet cool and didn't strain our acquaintance beyond the flimsy and pragmatic thing that it was. He said his peace, offered condolences, shook my hand, and was gone.

What salted the wound most was how few mourners appeared to mark their passage. I hadn't realized how much my parents kept to themselves. I had no brothers or sisters, no aunts or uncles. My parents, as far as I knew, were only children. Father's mother died before he could afford to bring her over. Father was gregarious but he didn't encourage intimacy, and Mother, so high-spirited and committed to parish organizations when we lived in Roosevelt, had apparently gotten lost in the new congregation. Only one person came out for both services, and that was Ada.

Each time she arrived late, hovered near the back, and left early, so that I never thanked her for coming.

Later, alone in my father's house, I felt like a servant entombed with Pharaoh in his pyramid, only Pharaoh lay elsewhere. The house seemed spooked, holding its breath, unsure how to respond to the changes, as though Father's death suggested its own limited usefulness. In the living room, with its cathedral ceiling and wall of glass looking out on a stand of pines, there hung a large painting of a violent ocean, and I stared at the green, black, and magenta waves. I wasn't even sure just where my parents were born: I knew the names of the cities but not of their streets.

What was this strange country from which they'd fled? Why was its fate so bleak, its identity so uncertain? While they spoke English to me, with each other they continued speaking Ukrainian, yet I felt no need to ask more about the place, until now. Occasionally my mother made *varenyky*, a kind of ravioli she said her mother had made for her, but I felt no more curious about the cuisine than I did about the history of wheat or the chemistry of cheese.

I poured myself a glass of red wine and sank back onto the couch. A cardinal landed on the empty feeder and I realized I'd forgotten to buy seed.

I remembered a game I'd played with Alex when, against my mother's wishes, I spent the night at the Kruks' apartment. It was called funeral parlor. In the narrow hallway near Ada's bedroom sat a huge pine trunk, large enough for us to crawl into, which had carried the family's possessions across an ocean and which was now used as a chest for clothes out of season. Alex and I took turns being dead. This was during the period when he still claimed he saw Ada's ghosts. Alex would lift the yellow lid and I'd slip into the soft bed scented with mothballs. Alex was funeral-director-cum-priest, spouting a spree of gibberish in benediction for the deceased. Meanwhile, I lay inside the trunk, imagining what it was like to be dead. Alex took his time with the service, mimicking the lugubrious Mass of childhood. I remember falling deep into myself and in the darkness hearing a scratching on the floor, and I imagined I saw fist-sized spiders with stiff legs coated in bristles and curling at the tips into enameled hooks baited with lips. Above me Alex improvised a liturgy. Then he sat on that lid so I couldn't get out and he wouldn't answer when I called, and as I struggled I remembered thinking that hell was a place where no one answered when you called.

The windows were open in my father's house but the street in our spacious suburban town was quieter than the cemetery. I'd been on my own in the city a long time. The city, with its relentless pressures, where even friends felt like competitors and lovers like predators. Despite the years of tennis and tests, competition was hateful to me, and I wondered how the world had gotten itself into this bind of relentless striving and measuring. In my third year of medical school, I felt stretched beyond my limits and no doubt I was vulnerable. I had late-night Catholic thoughts and slept poorly. I got up several times and stuck my head out the window to gape at the unblinking moon.

That was when I thought of Ada. Ada and I were connected. She'd come to both funerals. She not only knew me as a child, she'd loved me as a young man. I had avoided her so long because of our afternoon tryst; now I decided to call her. At best, I hoped she'd tell me something about my parents that might fill them out in my imagination and help me keep them there. And if she had nothing to add to the nothing I knew, at least I could spend a few minutes in the company of someone from the old life. I waited impatiently for morning.

Ada didn't seem surprised to hear from me and said I was welcome any time.

I got into my father's Lexus, now mine, and drove to Roosevelt.

The world, that funhouse mirror, refused to let me pass invisibly across its spectacular surface. It was something I might have liked, working quietly then disappearing, like those late afternoon clouds that materialize from nowhere as a huge mass, break into distinct shapes until the sky is suddenly crowded with sheep, then even as you stare at them dissolve to nothing in the fading light.

Eight years ealier Ada looked more like the woman I'd slept with than the sexless Sibyl seated before me now, and her eyesight had seemed fine.

She made no reference to our afternoon.

"You want to know about your parents?" she said after we'd sat down in the kitchen. "You already do. Good parents. I used to be jealous of your mother. You were such a fine boy. What else do you want?"

Was she speaking ironically? Or had she forgotten?

"They never told me anything," I said. "They almost never talked about the past. You know how they were. I couldn't even find where they grew up if I wanted to."

"Why would you want to?"

"Natural, don't you think?"

"For you, maybe. Not for Alex. My son never cared to hear about my world."

There were many things I might have said: that Alex fled the past with as much energy as Ada expended on dwelling in it; that he had enough trouble negotiating the present tense without further complications.

"I could never understand how you turned out like you did," she said.

"What do you mean?"

"Your parents had gone through the same things we did. In some ways worse. Your poor mother."

Pause. She looked at me—slyly, I thought.

"Worse?"

"They say she actually ate her sister."

The line came out sounding comic and I wondered if she was teasing. There was a shade, a dark rustle, of cruelty in her voice.

"I don't know if it's true. It was during the famine. You know the famine? In the thirties, millions died. There were many cases, and you heard all kinds of stories. Who knows what's true? One version was that she was in a village with her mother's family. The farmers' entire crop that year was gathered up by the communists and shipped to the cities. The villagers had run out of food and after they killed all the animals, the horses, the chickens, the dogs, the cats, they had nothing left. So they turned on each other. Your mother's younger sister died and your grandmother tried to keep your mother alive the only way she could. And she did. She kept her alive."

My mind recorded words that I played back much later, after I was alone.

My mother was a big woman, with a developed appetite. In my mind's eye I saw her making key lime in the mountains, clipping laundry on the porch in Roosevelt, vacuuming stairs in Fort Hills, her massive ankles visible under her housecoat, short of breath, jowly, smiling.

"And my father?"

She said:

"Peter was remarkable. Where did he get his energy? He was always working. Work redeems. Sweat of our brow. Even as a young man, he worked. For the Germans, when he had to. I saw him in his uniform. The brown shirt. They took all the boys, you know. It's not like he signed up. What choices did he have? He could have joined the underground. Some did. One of my brothers. But really, he was seventeen. If he hadn't, he would have been shot. Everyone understood."

I think until that moment I'd seen myself as basically a happy man. I had good luck in many things. My childhood had been the Black Pond and kick ball; Alex Kruk and Hattie Florentina; Fort Hills and tennis. Money had been tight, but the hardships had been handled and now that problem was behind me. Above all, I'd felt loved. Suddenly how flat my sense of things became.

And what had Ada told me, exactly? That my mother was a cannibal and my father a Nazi? Absurd even to utter such words, which sound unreal and oddly comic. I found myself yanked into the bloody whirlpool of mid-century battles. And where was the antidote to that?

I drove back to Fort Hills reeling. Images of death camps, heaps of corpses, and skeletal faces rolled through my mind. I tried remembering stray anti-Semitic remarks my parents may have made. None came to mind. This alone should have made me suspicious, I thought. Father had repressed himself. That's what he died of. We left the urban ghetto for a suburb that was heavily Jewish. Most of the other doctors in the building where my father had his office had been Jewish: Pinsky, Epstein, Kaysen, Applefeld. In high school the question simply didn't come up. My parents had changed their name from Verblud to Blud and I guess Nick Blud raised no eyebrows. The subject of my parents' nationality only came to my attention when a Ukrainian steel worker in Pennsylvania was arrested and accused of being a concentration camp guard.

Then I thought: maybe my father moved us to Fort Hills to throw everyone off track. Or he had done it out of guilt, to make up for the crimes committed in the old country. What if he were secretly being hunted even now? What if he had changed his name not in order to fit in so that he could pursue the dream unhampered but because he was afraid of being uncovered? What if at this moment the Nazi hunter Simon Wiesenthal, who was from Ukraine, was still on his trail: one day a call would come and I would find out even more horrible things. I would be interviewed on the news: son of a Jew killer uncovered living incognito in Boston! Pictures of me at twelve in my Boy Scout uniform in *People*: son of the Nazi doctor claims to be a radiologist!

Fortunately, a thousand details around the house kept me grounded in the moment.

3

Before heading back to Boston I decided to find Hattie Florentina. I needed to touch something from the past that hadn't been defiled.

Ada told me she now worked at a department store in one of the malls on Route 1.

How elastic America was, I thought, driving down the hideous highway. The strip had seemed so crowded years ago I couldn't imagine room for anything more. And yet more room had been found. New stores, bursting with computers, cell phones, and video games, had sprung up.

"Hattie?" I said to the round-faced blond woman behind the counter among the perfumes. "Remember me?"

There was no line; otherwise, she might have waved me on.

"Just between us, buddy, no."

"It's Nick, Hattie."

Her broad face was framed by a helmet of dead, straw-colored hair. When she smiled, I saw she'd been a smoker.

"Nick Blud."

She fingered the gold cross between her breasts.

"You know I thought I knew you. But you get that feeling a lot here. You think you see a face from the past but you don't have time, so you don't say anything."

"You have time now?" I asked.

"Break coming up. Wait a minute."

She turned and spoke to a young man at the register across from hers.

I looked toward the other side of the store, at the wall of televisions tuned to Oprah. The same face on a hundred silent screens mouthed urgent messages. At me.

"Come on," she said, touching me lightly on the wrist. I caught a glimpse of flesh rippling under the pink blouse.

We settled in a booth at the Friendly's next door and ordered coffee.

I told her about Boston. She joked about still being in New Jersey.

Then I told her my father had just died and she put her hand on mine. It was the first kind touch I'd had in a while.

After a few quiet minutes, I asked how her mother was.

Hattie smiled, "She cracks me up. Everything's a tragedy with her. It's made my life so much easier."

Then she added:

"You don't come to the old neighborhood."

"I know. Ever think about Paul?" I asked, remembering Alex's brother.

"Sometimes. Some days I can almost put my hands on us as we were when we were kids. But we sure didn't act like kids." Smiled again.

"Remember the wolf?"

She shrugged. "We were all wolves then."

"Once I found a box of photographs at a yard sale," I confessed. "I flipped through them and found a stack of pictures that looked like they were portraits of my grandparents. Swear to God. I had this impulse to buy them and bring them to my mother and ask her what she meant by selling the family pictures. I couldn't believe these weren't my relatives. It was crazy. It's like I'm always looking for my family."

She frowned.

"I mean, I think we're all related, more and more."

Instead of asking me to explain the outburst, she inquired:

"How's Alex? My mother says he's up in Boston with you."

Those who stayed were always more aware of those who'd left.

"Don't see him much. Not good. He drinks. Rehab. That sort of thing."

She nodded. "I miss Paul. I thought it was my fault he killed himself. Man, did I get it back for skipping his funeral. Like you won't believe."

She looked away. Pads of flesh rounded her once-sharp cheek bones, a small scar above her lip below her left nostril.

"I never finished college. Dropped out, worked at Gimbels, met somebody. Fell in love. Married. We lived in Phoenix, then Sarasota." She smiled, sipped her coffee, and went on.

"My husband was three years younger than me. Your age. But he looked a little like Paul. Same nose. Big shoulders. He was a pilot. It was romantic. I'd drive him to the airport, sometimes fly with him. We went places—Europe, Hawaii. Then he started doing a lot of coke. We'd do it together sometimes. But he kept doing it. He had to push hard, for work. When he finally hit bottom, it was almost as bad as though a plane had gone down. He stopped going out, lost his job, didn't return phone calls, hardly talked. He'd stare at the ceiling for days, not eating, barely breathing. One day I got back from work and he was in bed in his pajamas. Heart attack."

Her voice was steady, as though she were talking about someone else's life. "Ever been a generation that thought about death as much as we do? Strange—look around. This mall. There's so much. You know?"

"I know. But who ever thought up this mall idea, I hope he's in hell," I said. "Right?"

"You bet. You bet."

"Listen, come with me to the Reservation," I said.

She stopped. Was it over the line?

"In Watchung?" Smile. Watchung Reservation was a place kids went to make out. "When?"

"When you off?"

"Tomorrow's my day off," she said.

"Come."

"Sure."

The next afternoon I picked Hattie up at her apartment in Garwood.

A tapestry of leaves matted the sidewalk in front of her house.

We said hardly a word through the twenty-minute drive and it wasn't until we'd entered the forest that Hattie broke the silence:

"Look at the cardinal," pointing to a pine.

A sharp wind slid under my coat.

The moment felt charged and rich and I was frustrated at not being able to reach all that lay below the surface of my mind.

Her eyes had lost some luster; blue veins had surfaced in her hands like the roots of old trees. Her nose, once subtle, now looked splayed, as though she'd buried her face in her pillow too long. Yet, when she tucked in her chin and looked up at me, her lips still looked full.

The forest shivered with echoes: as kids we'd come here to drink Spañada, smoke pot, imagine a future characterized by the sort of recumbent, easy-going domesticity nobody I knew ever attained.

Foolish to have returned.

When she put her hand on my shoulder, I turned quickly, hooked my arms around her and melted into her. I lifted her skirt, my fingers raced straight for the center and found she hadn't worn panties. We lay on patchy ground, random tufts of grass sprouting here and there, and made love amid the puddles.

The moment I dropped her at her house, both of us silent, I felt it had been a dream. Never happened.

4

Back in Boston I fell into a depression. I couldn't bring myself to return to school. And I felt guilty about Hattie.

Distressed by my moping and hoping to distract me, my girlfriend at the time (another source of guilt, as I had long had my eye on Shelley) invited me to go with her to Spain. Her family was in coffee. They owned a million acres of fincas. Sandra used travel the way others did booze or drugs.

I agreed. I petitioned for and was granted a leave until the fall semester.

Outside Madrid, she insisted we attend a bullfight. The animals' energy surged like a current through the arena, animating even the drunks behind us. I thought of Hemingway, of *Death in the Afternoon* with its aggressive defense of this particular theater of cruelty, an homage to the gravitas of the blood rite. We watched four bulls slaughtered in two hours. Sandra settled for cheap thrills; if she could she would have licked the dead bull before it was hauled off by its feet, blood mapping the dust. The Cathedral of Burgos with its barnacled spires piercing the sky and the fiestas of Seville had bored her. I convinced myself I loved everything about her, from the way she brushed her teeth to how her jaw jutted, as though daring the world to take a swipe at it, to her strong nose and peppercorn eyes burning through the moment. She had such charms and gifts: she tap-danced, did magic tricks, and could speak backwards. She could repeat backwards whatever you said to her. In bed after sex, I'd make some intimate confession and hear it parroted: *Toh er'uoy dog*. And she made up words. *Zapatenku* became our code. Movies we didn't like were *zapatenku*, people about whom we had reservations were *zapatenku*. In Spain we drove everywhere, from Barcelona to Granada, taking the road up La Veleta, *la mas alta via in todo Europa*, where the subtlest ether flowed between us as we stood outside the car at the top looking at the unreal, shimmering landscape. We visited Salamanca, home of the philosopher Unamuno, rector of the university during the war. When the fascists showed up at the gates of the school, the philosopher, elegant in a beret, stood outside the entryway, facing down hundreds of soldiers with guns: "This is the temple of the intellect and I am its high priest. I forbid you to enter," he announced. They entered, arresting him—and where were they now?

Yet my parents had disappeared as though they'd never been on earth in the first place. And even as I watched the bulls go down, I kept thinking of my father in uniform and my mother's terrible hunger.

After ten days, my soon-to-be-ex was ready to go home. I accompanied her to the airport in Madrid and waved at her plane as it took off. Even before it disappeared into the clouds I knew I'd never see her again.

Still numb, I returned to the city where I bought a train pass, and over the next days I traveled through France and down along the Italian coast. It turned into one of those journeys you can take only in your twenties, when you're still open enough to the world for it to appear personally responsive.

Had circumstances been different, I might have visited the old country, seeking the sites whose afterlife cast such shadows. But things were not normal. Technically, my parents and I were Soviet citizens, and while it would not have been likely, I was liable to be arrested if I "returned"—to a place I'd never been. Ada's revelation certainly didn't inspire me in that direction and everything in my education inclined me west.

After years of deliberate living, I let chance lead. I traveled on hunches and intuitions and criss-crossed Europe several times, thinking nothing of going south to Sicily, then doubling back to Aix. Yet the trip never felt anything less than predestined: everywhere I went I felt connected, as though I were being passed like a baton from runner to runner. The goal of my wanderings, which I'd never have acknowledged at the time, was redemption, and countless cunning strangers took part in the process. A well-dressed Armenian on the train from Madrid insisted I pray at a temple on Aegina, so I did. There I fell in with a lovely South African woman named Martine, who mourned her country's plight on my shoulder so charmingly I thought for a while my next stop would be Johannesburg. We camped on a beach long enough to befriend the octopus fishermen who gathered each dawn to scoop up the creatures they then softened by pounding against the rocks sixty times before delivering them fresh to the market a few blocks away. We scorned the hotels and mocked the German ladies whose correct dresses contrasted comically with the plain garb of the locals. Then we visited Paris and I got drunk and lost my glasses and the next day in the Louvre I missed the Mona Lisa, but I remember blue Martine in a kerchief waving good-bye from the balcony of the flea-bag hotel where we'd spent half the night killing lice and the other half making love, and where I left her to continue my pursuit alone.

North, in Narvik, I watched the churning of Europe's strongest whirlpools; in Oslo I searched out the haunts of Knut Hamsun, a favorite writer of my mother's and, I told myself, a notorious fascist; in Switzerland I glimpsed Matterhorn and hiked the Simplon Pass, where Wordsworth had gone two centuries before; in Florence I saw the doors of Hell, sat in the surreal ambiance of the Piazza della Signoria, and wandered around Fiesole. In Assisi, someone told me about a Ukrainian church on the outskirts of Rome, and I noted its address.

In Rome I found a cheap pension not far from Stazione Termini in an Ethiopian neighborhood where I swapped stares with a man who claimed to be a witch doctor and who gave me the *mal'ochio*. The next day I read a story in the *Tribune* about an Ethiopian who'd been attacked and set on fire by a neighborhood street gang.

One night, at a bar near the Pantheon, I sat down next to a thin monk in a brown robe who looked like Cardinal Richelieu.

He was nursing a Campari soda while watching a soccer game on television. When a team scored he blurted out, "Way to go, boys." Hearing his accented English, I felt emboldened and asked whom he favored in the World Cup.

"Italians, naturally. But they haven't a chance against the Argentineans. *Sono cativi, no?* "

It turned out he was a Ukrainian from Canada. The coincidence delighted him and he began speaking quickly. Destiny, to be sure. Did I know there was a large community of us in Rome? Oh yes, oh yes. For centuries. Didn't I know Gogol had come here to die? Yes yes, our people have close ties, very close.

"You should come stay with us," he said, throwing out his arms.

"And where would that be?"

"The monastery's in the hills of Grottoferrata. About thirty kilometers outside the city. On Lake Nemi. Across from the Pope's summer villa, " he added as though that was bound to be an inducement.

To my surprise, I accepted. The next morning I met him in front of a convent near the Coliseum and together we drove out in his battered red Fiat, climbing the narrow roads, passing fruit stands and farmers with forks over their shoulders and goats at the edge of the road watching us.

The setting was oleanders surrounding an eighteenth-century palazzo with fig trees in the back where sheep grazed, tended by a monk who sang snatches of Mario Lanza tunes. Olive trees scrambled over the hills like an army of hunchbacked green skeletons through which, at sunset, swallows flitted. Every facet of the landscape had a burnished maturity masking a wildness. Ripeness is all, and all that was around me was ripe. Here was a place Ada's ghosts might have spread out. I was told that from my room, on a clear day, you could see Cicero's theater.

I never found it, though this may have been because I spent little time in my room.

Instead, I stalked the grounds restlessly, passing among chickens and the strutting rooster, the cage housing three feral homosexual dogs, down to the beehives, and the field beyond where some afternoons I took a bottle of wine and a book.

I tried attending at least one of the seven daily services, joining the half-dozen monks ranging in age from late twenties to early sixties. During our modest dinners, which consisted of tomatoes, onions, buttered potatoes, and boiled chicken, we listened while one of them read from the lives of the Desert Fathers, a text I promptly rechristened "Where's the Dessert, Fathers?"

The monks themselves were variously gifted, peculiar, and friendly, and whenever they had time they took me on day trips, mainly to neighboring monasteries. Visiting a Camadalusian monastery in Tusculum I heard a white-haired abbot shouting to a farmer driving a tractor: "Put the pedal to the metal!" and was told he'd once worked narcotics on the New York City police force.

Brother George, from what was then still Yugoslavia, liked guns, and many afternoons we'd hear him shooting from the roof, allegedly over the heads of the kids he insisted were trying to torch the monastery. Sometimes he invited me to join him on guard duty.

Down the hall from me lived an eminent Cardinal whose story was swathed in romance and mystery. Arrested by the communists immediately after the war, he'd spent seventeen years in Siberian exile and was only released in the sixties through the intercession of President Kennedy. He was a large man, with a full face and a long white beard, aloof and unapproachable, or so he seemed. He was attended by a slim, sloe-eyed nineteen-year-old nun, also from Yugoslavia. The only time I ever heard him speak outside Mass was at a dinner celebrating his eightieth birthday, when he asked, in stentorian tones, for more cake.

While most of my two months there passed serenely, I was surprised when one evening at dinner the guest I'd been told to expect was someone I'd seen before. Again his appearance was prefaced with whispers and rumors, though this time they insinuated our visitor was a rarefied yet worldly mystic who made an annual pilgrimage through Italy.

At five-thirty I descended into the basement of the palazzo where we dined on chickens from the monks' own coop, hacked and plucked for us by the nuns, along with honey from their hives and wine from the nearby village of Frascati. The Cardinal ate alone in his room.

Most of the other monks were already huddling around the diminutive figure at their center when I arrived. As I took my place at the far end of the table I recognized Anton, the poet.

I'd seen him last a decade or so earlier, back home, tutoring an unhappy crowd in the free verse innovations of Whitman. And I had read his *Ambassador of the Dead*, which had given me a glimpse of all that Ada had been through in the old country. He was now in his seventies, but despite a certain tension evident around the lips, Anton looked remarkably unchanged. His dress was vaguely nineteenth-century bohemian: he wore an embroidered Japanese vest and carried a cane. I introduced myself and told him who my parents were. His thick eyebrows rose. He seemed delighted at the coincidence.

"The doctor. I knew your father slightly. Dead? So sorry. Knew your mother, too. A little. Even mentioned her in something I wrote once. She was a friend to Ada Sich. You also know Ada? Kruk's the name now."

I told him I'd seen her recently. What I did not say right away was that it was her news about my parents that had sent me hurtling around the world.

After dinner he suggested a walk. A fading sun spilled amber light over the pines rimming the lake.

"This is where *The Golden Bough* opens. You remember? The book that inspired *The Wasteland*. You don't know the story? Who knows what anybody knows anymore. Yet here you are, in the middle of it!

"That's why people used to come to Europe—because they heard these stories and they wondered how to connect with them. They needed to see for themselves.

"The air!" He patted his flat chest "You can make a life in such a place. Somewhere on this lake below is the grove of Diana. Legend is the place was guarded by a priest who kept his sword always in hand. He was waiting for his successor, who was supposed to announce himself by killing him.

"Place was dedicated to Diana by Orestes, son of Agamemnon. From the Trojan war? His father was murdered by Clytemnestra? Electra, his sister?"

He looked to see if I was following.

I shrugged. "Sort of."

"He'd killed a Crimean king—that's where Ada summered, you know, the Crimea. Orestes stole an image of the goddess Diana that he carried to Italy. And it was a bough from a tree in Diana's grove Aeneas used to reach the land of the dead. Aeneas, you remember, founded Rome," he added, not trusting my American education.

Around us fell shadows from pines that may have been distant relations to the very trees Anton was talking about. The sun had slipped behind the hills yet the twilight air remained hot. There were no cars on the road. In the stillness and clarity I felt I was walking outside my body.

"Orestes, Aeneas, Diana. It's the old world, fading fast. That's why you've come. You're looking for origins. Count yourself lucky for even knowing to look."

I then repeated what Ada had told me about my parents.

He listened without saying a word. An old truck filled with hay sputtered past us and we stopped to watch a group of men scything grass on a hillside while sheep wandered nearby.

"It's not impossible. Your mother might have done that. Of course she wouldn't have talked about it. Her sister was a sacrifice ... to you."

My heart quickened.

"To you, of course, because what else but an instinct for life? Sometimes what people do to preserve has the opposite effect on the next generation.

"But your father. No. Impossible. I knew him slightly. I remember him as *Ostarbeiter,* a forced laborer. He worked on a chicken farm, as I recall. Nazis used a lot of people that way. Not a soldier. Ada's wrong."

He stopped and fixed me in his soft stare.

"Worse. Sounds like she's lying. Why would she want to hurt you?

"I knew people who belonged to the German divisions. Thousands did. We have blood on our hands. No denying. No denying. You should find out about it. Don't hide. Some became monsters. Your father wasn't one.

"War perverted a lot of people. They were ready for it, waiting to be perverted. Ada's husband Lev. I remembered him from home—I thought he was a solid character, and see how he behaved."

I couldn't quite take in the news.

"What can I do?"

"Nothing. The sins of the fathers. Old story. Bible says it takes three generations to dissolve. What do I know? You can't do a thing about the dead except to pray for them, if you're a believer.

"I'm not saying don't wonder what your father did. Do. But have your own life. Don't get trapped. The past can become an evasion, an escape, easier to deal with than what's around you.

"Tell me about Ada."

By the time we'd circled the lake, it was dark. Brother George greeted us at the gate, smiling, rifle in hand.

That night a heat wave trapped us under its bell jar and I couldn't sleep. I rose, opened the shutters, pulled up the window, then shut it when mosquitoes began zig-zagging in. I remembered counting fireflies at Black Pond, waiting for Viktor to return.

I decided to get some air, so I walked down the stairs and stepped out the palazzo gates, crossed the road, and plunged into the forest where the pungent pines burned invisibly. I began walking fast, as though I had a destination. Eventually I broke into a run.

Crickets carried night on their wings and someone was shooting stars into the lake, though maybe it was kids with bottle rockets. I didn't know where I was running; I felt driven by a desire to find Diana's grove where I might fight the priest and pluck a bough that would give me passage to the land of the dead. Did I believe Anton? Ada? Why would either lie? Soon I was sweating, scratched, and lost. Was this what it meant to be an American, this constant uncertainty, looking over your shoulder at nothing—miles and centuries of nothing—and not knowing what was ahead? The darkness was deep as the day had been bright. Exhausted, I decided to turn back. I needed to face the present. The past was broken; it would remain broken. I would get no satisfaction from it; nor could I repair it. The most I could do was my work.

As I groped slowly up the wooded hill I saw a camp fire in the distance off to the side. I headed in its direction. My heart pounded. Who would it be? Gypsies? The priest of Diana? Nearing it, I saw three figures sitting in a half circle with their backs to me. One must have heard me because he leaped up, whirled around, and cried out:

"Who's there?"

His accent sounded English.

"Don't worry," I called back, drawing closer.

The other two stood and turned toward me. They were wearing shorts, which undercut whatever else about them might have been menacing.

They were men about my age, and as I entered the compass of

their fire I noticed backpacks leaning against the trunks of the trees.

"Man, don't do that, mate," said the first one.

"Sorry," I apologized, explaining myself to what turned out to be three Australians hitchhiking through Europe. They offered me some cheap wine and I took a swig before saying I needed to get back to the monastery. Dragging up the hill all at once I felt very tired and old.

The next day Brother George told me Anton had left at dawn.

A week later I decided that, tonic as it was, the monastic life wasn't for me. I missed too many things found only in the Romes of earth, whose lights teased me nightly as I paced the roof of the palazzo, accompanied by Brother George and his pet rifle. Above all, I missed women. I saw the world through carnal eyes and felt no way above the play of flesh and bone. My heart was a heart of eros and dust and if one day it is judged for its allegiances, let it stand clear.

And so I left the hills and returned to Stazione Termini, where I caught a train to Paris and from there flew out of Orly back to New York.

In Fort Hills, I pored over my parents' papers like an IRS agent. Over days I studied hundreds of photographs, passports, citizenship papers, and report cards in various languages: Romanian, Polish, Ukrainian, and German. Nothing looked incriminating. What was the truth of what had occurred in the old country? I thought of my mother bringing me to school, playing Monopoly with me. I remembered Father driving us to the mountains, Cape May, taking me on trips through the city, looking for Viktor. I thought of seeing the new house for the first time, the excitement with which my parents told me we were leaving Roosevelt. And how was any of this changed by things that happened before I was born? No easy answers came; few hard ones, either. My parents were gone, and here I was, with an uncertain legacy, alone. Whatever may have been true in what Ada and Anton had told me, my sense of the past was changed. I would have to live with doubt. I wouldn't let my desire for sentimental simplicities obscure the shadowy labyrinths of that invisible world.

I threw away most of what I found; a few things I saved, who knows why? For the kids. I kept my father's instruments and made his stethoscope my own. I put the house on the market and when it sold I bought a small condo in Boston. That fall I reentered medical school, which I finished in due time.

5

The flare of a lighter brought me back to Roosevelt and the present.

"You still smoke?" I asked stupidly, watching Ada light a Benson and Hedges.

Whose breasts I held, whose tongue I tasted.

Shuffling cars along the snowy street sounded like horse-drawn wagons and I let myself imagine we'd slipped out of the nightmare and back into the nineteenth century.

"Shocked?"

"It's the worst."

"Nonsense. Think of those lovely old Chinese who smoked for seventy years. Four packs a day. Unfiltered. Health is a complicated concept. Nothing to do with smoking and diet. Eat more. You'll be happier."

"You said I was fat."

"Aren't you? Anyway, I can't see. It was just a guess."

"Adriana ..."

"You're boring. The other day," she went on, stubbing out her cigarette, "in religion class, we were talking about the orders of the Seraphim, and Father Myron said that powerful as angels are, God is always surprising them. And people surprise them too. People can even surprise God. Almost. I wonder if Father Myron knows what he's talking about. So many priests killed in the war, you wonder about the ones who survived. Not necessarily pick of the litter. You know that during the war we had a guardian angel? I used to see him all the time. Red wings. I pointed him out but Viktor couldn't see. Viktor saw other things. Once he told me about a forest where trees ate people."

She leaned back in the chair.

"Why don't you go to church? In the old country, not allowed, we found a way. Here you have freedom and you don't.

"It's not supposed to make you feel good," she said. "Just give thanks. Sometimes I wish I'd been shot by the communists. I've gone to church years without grasping the service. Not before Vatican II and not now. What are they doing there? I tell myself it doesn't matter, I'm there for God. And what good has that done? I could do nothing to stop the war, or save my mother."

Adriana stood up and felt her way to a bureau in the corner where she nimbly opened a drawer and pulled out a quartered sheet of paper from an envelope, which she handed me, saying Anton had sent it—a poem he'd translated by someone named Rudenko.

"Viktor read it to me once," Ada shrugged. "Read it again," she said, settling back down.

The title, unpromisingly, was "Spring":

No delight in the riot of trees
Sweeping green slopes and groves.
Why deny it? Young, I counted too many
Of them rising from graves.

Green we sank to our knees,
Wounded, not begging the killers.
Boys matured into maples;
Inside the poplars, girls whispered.

No delight in the sprouting of shoots—
I know what nourished the roots.
I'll order the nightingale
to publish my griefs.

Let her drink the waters of dawn,
In her throat refine them to song—
And all that followed my autumn
Rehearse for a late-blooming youth.

"Nice. What should I do with it?"

"With a poem? It does something to you.

"As a girl," Adriana added, her long fingers raising a cage over her heart, "I expected to grow up a European. You don't even know what that is. The name Stefan Zweig mean anything to you?"

"No."

"Too bad. Because I knew his work and I can sing 'It's a Long Way to Tipperary.' You don't know much about your culture or your people. Eat more. You want to be an American. But what's an American? Everybody comes from somewhere. Centuries later, they're still from somewhere else first. A lot remember. The Irish remember. English remember. Africans remember. Koreans. Jews. You should too. Part of you will always stay foreign to me. And I'll never understand your America."

She tapped her fingers on the chair's arm.

"What's that mean?"

"There are names. Traditions. Franz Werfel. We should go back to the old country and claim what they stole."

"Not from me."

"True. You inherited your world from us," she muttered.

"Some I've made myself."

"What is a self?" she sighed.

This was the way she must have talked to Alex.

An ancient oppressiveness settled over us—a peculiarly Slavic mix of hopelessness, the weight of the past drifting down in invisible webs, raining from the sky in soft, sticky lattices that snared and smothered, leaving me feeling action was impossible.

My mother told me once about running into Ada outside church:

"I got angry at her," she said. "She was standing there, talking to that Nina of hers. I told her: 'Enough ghosts. Leave her alone, Nina. Go home! Enough.' Ada stewing in her griefs can't see the world. It makes me mad. When we were in the neighborhood, she never learned the lives of people around her, except for Mrs. Florentina, whom she couldn't avoid. And her men. Stuck in her self, she missed her chance. She had a chance. God gives us that. She could have taken her life back. Next door lived a man dying of

Goucher's disease, who could have used company. Around the corner was a girl with leukemia whose mother was paralyzed from an accident. She could have helped Blind Roman or Teta Hernandez. So many calling, and all she heard was Nina!"

"Now, Slava," Father said. "She's had it harder than we have."

She coughed into a yellowed handkerchief.

"Enough. What about Alex?"

"A minute," she said, her voice phlegmy. "Believe me, no hurry. You realize that. All that racing for money, love, children, thinking you had to, and? Did any of it matter or do my children good? No, Nicholas, you listen: there is no hurry. Not now. Not ever.

"I want to talk," she continued. "Tell me about you. Your wife. She's Jewish, isn't she?"

I looked at this incurably strange woman.

"Alex told me. He never met her, but he said the two of you were happy."

"We are."

"That's good. Unusual, you know: a Jew and a Ukrainian."

"My wife says the same."

"Isn't that funny? She's right. Does she know your history?"

She seemed to suppress a giggle.

"If you mean the stories you told me, sure."

"Good. Marriages can't bear secrets."

6

I met Shelley in medical school but it wasn't until years later, in Washington, while staying at the Holiday Inn in Dupont Circle for a conference on HMOs, that we had our first extended conversation.

I'd noticed her early, back in Boston. There was something clean and crisp about her face, a feeling of precision—she looked well-made, from the black hair cut straight across her forehead to the strong chin—some chins simply fell off a face without finishing it, while this one ended cleanly, like a paragraph.

I'd see her in a classroom, a hallway, the street. Each time I struggled to contrive a meeting but before I could put it in words either she or I would be swept along to the next obligation. So it went for years, until she became a curious fixture in a fantasy life enfeebled by the hours we kept—she was like a beautiful garden you pass daily on your way to work, beside which you linger, hoping the owner might step out and invite you in.

Our careers had so far traveled parallel tracks that changed course only in D.C. That day, we happened to sink down next to each other, into plush green lounge chairs in the hotel lobby, to consult our coffees before plunging into the conference.

She wore a pale blue cashmere sweater and pale lipstick.

I said hello. She nodded without looking up. She later told me she avoided making eye contact, but I was too sleepy to notice. Yet I felt instinctively challenged and kept tossing lines in her direction.

"Dull conference."

"Really? I think there are some great panels today," she countered.

"Like what?" I asked.

She looked away. As she stared in the direction of the check-in counter, where a woman with two young girls spoke animatedly to the clerk, I again admired her profile.

When she turned to face me, I felt in a flush that she not only knew who I was, but that she had something to say to me. She held my eyes in her gaze a few seconds.

Finally, in a voice that smiled as it sliced, she replied: "Look. Let me just say this."

"Sure."

"Your parents were murdering my parents in the old country."

"What?"

I looked at the woman walking away from the counter, girls in tow.

"You're Ukrainian, aren't you?" And so our relationship began on this surreal note, with my wife-to-be accusing me of anti-Semitism by default. It turned out she'd been avoiding me all these years. I don't remember what I said to ingratiate myself, but before we left for our conferences I'd extracted a promise that we'd continue the conversation.

That night, over drinks in the hotel bar, she told me why she was so aware of these things.

"My mother had cousins who died in Auschwitz," she explained. Her intensity reminded me of the Kruks.

"Have you ever been to Poland?"

"Don't think I want to. For years I wished my mother would assimilate—my father's Italian, from Brooklyn—but then I thought: look at the Jews of Germany. Her family had been there since they were expelled from Spain. They'd become German. Almost. By then they didn't know who they were. And what difference did it make? They were never German to the Germans."

"So are you orthodox?" I asked.

"You don't know much, do you? Most goyim know nothing about Jews except what they see on TV. Nobody's fault, really. Everyone hurries down his little path and nobody stops at the spots off the map. We live in ghettoes. How many black people do you know?"

"One. So what have you heard about my people?"

"Pogroms. Nazis. The usual. And you?" Shelley asked.

"Usurers. Communists. The media," I countered.

"The hardest thing. Always say the hardest thing," she urged.

"OK. How come you hear about the Holocaust all the time, but never the Famine?"

"Go and tell the world about it," she said.

"The community thinks the information's suppressed," I said.

I had never spoken about this with anyone. Indeed, I hadn't realized how much old world lore I'd picked up on my own simply by scanning the paper. "For years people didn't believe the country my parents came from existed. Papers called it Russia. It's like if you were from Boston and moved to Europe and people called you Canadian because people in Canada also speak English. It drove people nuts."

"You start down this road and who knows where it ends?" she said.

"Fine, let's stop. We're Americans," I offered.

"You're right. This is interesting. I've heard your people were the worst."

I too had heard this. "And every American owned slaves."

"The point is, a lot of Jews feel Slavs are anti-Semitic."

"What about the Jews in the Communist Party? There were more of them there than there were collaborators."

"That's what your dear mother taught you? Interesting."

"My mother didn't teach me any of it. Here's what I read, though: Jews came to Eastern Europe when Western Europe wouldn't have them. The Russians, who controlled my parents' country, created the Pale where the Jews were allowed to settle. They put them at odds with the native population, pitting people against each other so they couldn't see who was using them. All the tricks of Imperial Rome. Anyway, what's Russia? Who were the czars? There's little that's Russian about the Romanovs. They intermarried so much they were more German and Danish than Russian. The Gottorp-Holstein dynasty," I said.

"You think of Jews as coming from elsewhere, not native. You view them as a 'them' in relation to your people, whom you see as 'natives.' That's what I mean. After all these centuries. That's anti-Semitic."

"What should I say to that? I mean, my people? I think of them as a 'them' too. Americans, that's who my people are," I said.

"We don't live on air. We have roots. Even now can you admit your complicity? Just once?"

"My complicity? My complicity? I grew up in New fucking Jersey!" I felt outraged and confused.

I finally broke the silence. "So are you reformed?"

"Don't change the subject," her voice was sharp with experienced anger. We glared at each other. "Why is it so hard for you to say these things?"

"Because I'd like to think I'm better than I am," I said.

"You know," she said, backtracking, "I think everything changed after the Holocaust. For everyone. Forget the Famine. This is how I see it. The Holocaust and Hiroshima ended the century. The millennium. We're in a whole new era. Don't you feel it? Something strange. Europe's becoming one tribe, and we have all this electronic stuff. It's not about science, it's transformation."

"What's this got to do with what we were talking about?"

"The old values have lost their power. Everybody starts over."

There was a disturbance at the counter. A guest was complaining about a musician rehearsing next door.

Her tone changed. "Listen, I have to ask. You feel different because of what your family went through?"

"Are you kidding?"

"Stuff that bothers other people never worries me. For years I've been trying to figure out this competition angle. My parents pushed me. But their stories told me that everything can change overnight. Pasts like ours make most of what people worry about seem crazy."

We spent much of our time during that conference in private sessions. It was as though I'd found someone with whom I'd been speaking for years without knowing it, and while the talking wasn't always fun, it felt like a compulsion, the completion of something, as though a story whose strands had been knotted before I was born were finally loosened.

Shelley surprised both of us by agreeing to see me back in Boston. We dated for nearly a year before she brought me home to meet her mother.

"Don't tell her you're Ukrainian," she said.

"What should I say?"

"Just tell her you're a doctor from New Jersey."

"Will that work?"

"No."

Of course not. Life with my extended family has been its own journey, but the history of our mutual accommodations doesn't belong here. I've mentioned it only because it was Ada who set this train in motion, and it is to Ada in Roosevelt that we must return.

The Invisible World

1

" . . . and they jumped out of the plane together, only his parachute didn't open . . ."

"Ada."

I began sneezing.

Silence. Downstairs the dog howled an unearthly sound, and the radiator rattled, and cold bolted through rotten casements.

"Some days I feel the life inside me move like wind and think: I'll always be here," she said, lighting another cigarette. "Others come and go, but I'm here forever."

Her long face in the shadows seemed to grow sad.

"I'm not," I said, standing up. "Either we see Alex now, or I'm leaving and you get what you need from somebody else."

She seemed to take this in.

"Help," she finally said, struggling to rise, and I leaned forward, grabbing her elbow, choking down the perfume fertilizing a topsoil of smoke.

Past the eyes of horses and hounds, then down the hall, stacked with telephone directories and yellow pages towering above my head.

"What are these?"

"The books? Viktor collected them." Her left arm probing ahead like an insect's antenna.

She pushed open the door to her bedroom, and as once before, I followed her in.

Same greenish brown floral print paper, darkened and stained with smoke and time. Thick curtains covered high, shaded windows. Air even richer than in the living room, as though a jar crammed with gherkins and petals, photos and rinds, had moldered in a hothouse for years—a bath of wax slowly congealing, a cube of amber embedded with insects and limbs. A walnut-veneered dresser, whose surface was covered with make-up, brushes, pencils, crumpled Kleenex, and a crab claw, against the wall, crowned by a mirror. Even the blind wear make-up.

The bed was placed to the side of the door, so it was in the mirror that I first glimpsed him, stretched fully dressed over the spread. Fox the hounds were after. Shaggy face damp. Stone-washed jeans and a white shirt stained the color of festering strawberries. I remembered dabbing a finger against his bleeding arm after he'd been struck by the snakes, and I hurried over, bent low, and put my hand to his forehead. Warm. I'd assumed he was dead.

I looked at Ada, who stood in the doorway, awaiting orders.

The ions in the room felt highly charged: dead air shrill, as though out of sight an invisible bird screeched.

"What?" I bent down and tore open his shirt. Milk scum skin.

Belly six inches below his nipples cut ragged as lips, like someone had taken a bite out of him—or, likelier, slit him with a serrated knife.

"Ada?" Heart sprinting, fingers touching his hand, wrapping his wrist, palming his chest.

He was dead. Recently. Larval face puckered. Hair greasy. Eyes shut. Green chenille stained purple.

The Catskills, attacked by the snakes. The Kruko, standing up to the world in Warninenco Park, running down the streets of Roosevelt, picking a fight at the Plough.

"Ada!"

She remained near the door, stiff, face aimed toward the window across the room, alongside the mirror. Earrings chimed.

"Late last night. Morning, really. He woke us up, ringing," she said. "Babbling, drunk. A fight. Something stupid. You know how he's been. Hospitals. Homes.

"God. My God." She spoke slowly. Her tone was soft, philosophical. "What did I do? He'd been in Boston. Called twice a month. Then Mrs. Kupchak said she'd seen him in Roosevelt. I asked Father Myron, but he didn't know. What could I do? Send Viktor?

"I waited. He'd come. Lord knows where from, or sleeping where. With who.

"And he did. He couldn't talk. Mumbled. Viktor helped him here. Didn't see. Blood under the coat. Not at first." She gestured to the floor at the foot of the bed. I stayed crouched at Alex's side, listening, smelling sweat, smoke, and feces.

"He cried. I stroked his hair. Long, sweaty, dirty hair. Disappearing sickness. That should have told me.

"I didn't know what. I wasn't frightened. I squeezed his hand and he brought it to his mouth and began sucking my fingers."

"You should have called the police. The hospital."

"I couldn't. My son came home to die. Why should I give him to strangers?

"He disgusted me. So I decided. Knew. Easy.

"I had Viktor find the Valium Hlib prescribes, which I never use. It's there. I crushed them all in water …"

I got up and began pacing the plum carpet.

She sidled over to the bed.

"He was alive when I got here," I said.

I looked at her in her black dress and the sweater with its mother of pearl buttons—her lips pale, face cracked and dry as August earth. Still dignified, even beautiful.

"That's why I couldn't let you in. Death certificates for the living? I didn't think it would take so long. That you'd hear him breathing. I still do."

Looking out the frosted pane at the familiar facades, I saw the snow slowing.

After a brief pause, she added:

"Don't be sentimental, Nicholas. You know people."

Voice flat.

After a long time, I opened my eyes.

Ada now sat beside Alex, hand on his forehead. Blind eyes open, mouth resigned. Nativity's sequel.

Viktor shuffled in.

"She's tougher than Truman," he said. "Drink?"

That was why Ada'd reached out to me. She knew I would do it. How not? I called St. Mary's. I phoned the police. I persuaded Lieutenant Mike Kronsky—the tough cop who'd once saved Alex and myself from being beaten by a gaggle of hoods in the park, now paunchy and nearing retirement and smoking a cigar and who remembered Paul but not Alex—that I'd been in the neighborhood visiting when Alex staggered in. I said I'd examined him quickly, that he died before our eyes, that everything was as in order as a situation like this ever gets. Alex had already taken the drugs before stumbling in and had died not long ago.

Naturally there would be an autopsy—it was after all a murder. But no one would follow this case far: the Kruks were obscure people from an obscure country living shadowy lives. It didn't feel good, but it should have felt worse. I didn't want to see Ada punished further. Alex had bled to death; drugs just numbed the pain.

What is a mother? The source of life, a nest of love, a furnace of warmth, the heart's first tutor and patron saint of the emotions? Possibly. A mother is Eve, Sarah, Ceres, Cybele, Mary, and Mother Earth—the sea, the moon, and more. Much more. Medea. A Maenad. A cannibal. Mother as murderess; eater of children.

Death, a writer once observed, is the dark backing a mirror needs if we are to see anything. I like to imagine Alex back in seventh grade again looking at the new map of the old world, and I overhear his teacher, tutored in sensitivity training, straining to pronounce his name.

The snow had stopped by the time I stepped outside. The sidewalks hadn't been cleared yet and I had to walk carefully. Under a street lamp a skunk nosed round some boxes, a mirror of the black and white night. Cars swooshed, slow brushes on a snare. Cold. Christmas lights in the windows. A few blocks down the stores began. I remembered running along this street, away from Alex, past Kolber Sladkus, hair salons, strip joints. Gone. I stopped before an Indian video store and watched the old clerk shelving boxes: what did he dream of, white winter nights?

I doubt Ada knew a day's rest in her life—though she found ways of escaping, minutes at a time, paying for the respite with decades of shame. The shame of the Kruks, and their struggle, were more mine than I understood—in a world at peace, we carried in our bodies memories of war.

2

Shelley told me this: Mystics claim that when Moses met God on Mount Sinai he was shown the Torah, a text of black fire inscribed on white flame. What he carried down with him was a translation of the flickering black letters we know today as the commandments; but the real Torah, the true law, what God revealed to Moses and to Moses alone, was in fact what had been blazoned in white, below the black letters. The black fire was what was told; the white fire was what had not been told, a text every one must decipher for himself, striving from lifetime to lifetime to read a little further, recognizing the future as the only road open for approaching the past.

Alex's death may have had its source in Ada's mother love. Her physicality and overwhelming fantasy life a psychiatrist might describe as functional schizophrenia couldn't have helped. But what doctor would know or understand the history behind the Kruks' story? Fatherless, Alex never learned to move beyond the veil of inherited images.

And Adriana was in many ways heroic. She'd seen her city flattened by bombs, all but erased from the planet. Only heroes spend lifetimes refusing to forget or betray their homes. Has anyone troubled to track down the men who destroyed her world? But it's not my aim to trespass on the grounds kept by my colleagues. There are psychological explanations for her actions and maybe there are historical ones.

So Ada Kruk, nee Sich, born in the city of Resurrection, on the river Memory, returns once more with her family to the Black Sea. The day is cloudy; waves battle the shore. This time Ada keeps the red scarf on. She turns and looks at the white house hanging above the dune, gabled and framed by prodigal oaks. Or maybe they're poplars. In the apparitional light of a white sun, bleached and blinding, she sees her father and mother bent over the roses rambling down the weathered fence. The wind knocks her father's hat off. He gives chase and she follows, but the wind keeps yanking it away until they disappear around the corner and behind the house.

Pan Micho, the beekeeper's cat, pounces on her white patent leather shoe, but before she can hoist him up, he too runs off after a necklace of dried seaweed sidewinding through the air like a flying serpent. Her brothers and sisters race in a line over the dunes.

She wears a child's body, yet she is not a child. She views the world through ancient eyes, a sibyl reading in the faces of those appearing before her the hard map of destiny, down to the last burst vessel, herniated disc, and corroded artery. The beach is a magic theater, a stage of sand. She strains to register each breeze and transcribe every current of air, knowing this moment holds the next in a fist that opens and closes: around her a million hands shut and sigh like mouths depositing fragments of the future onto the miles of sand.

The naked redhead swimming in the sea is her father's mistress. Ada frowns. Whore! she wants to shout. No—to what end? Why add to the rage gathering in the clouds overhead? She hadn't noticed them seventy years ago. So her father had a mistress, so what? He must not have known how else to ask for what he needed. The knowledge would surely have scarred her mother, but history overtook domesticity, and countless private lives and stories never found their natural end. So she carried her father's betrayals inside her—and not his alone. There were the soldiers who raped, who murdered, the men who gave them orders, who seemed to have escaped justice, the men who abused her over the decades. The lying gypsy: son of Genghis indeed. And what had been their reward? Only Anton the poet was spared the lash of her half-conscious judgment. Anton, who took her to hear *La Boheme*, who gave her his sad little story, on which the foolish fellow had worked so hard he couldn't hear the world laughing at him for his troubles. She remembered sleeping alongside her aunt's dogs and standing to have her portrait painted.

It occurs to her that everything has been her fault: in the suffering around her she was the common denominator. Her brothers and sisters, her parents, her sons. Had she been born elsewhere, in another body, life might have seemed the gift some claimed it was. She was Medea, Medusa, the Maenads: whoever stepped inside her circle could count on being blasted by violence, by the split atom of evil concealed in things as a potentiality. It had been her destiny to unleash it, as though she were the breaker of isotopes, the nuclear trigger.

Seeing Slava approach, a skinny braided girl, queen of the winds, she wants to shout: No. Stop!

Blood drips from her friend's mouth. No! Turn around. Go away! I'm a curse.

It's as though she had summoned a meeting or thrown a party at her embassy, the embassy of the dead. They were all returning: her lost brothers and sisters, son Paul, the terrible husband. The sun strikes each figure as it tramples over the dunes and bathes them in brightness: she looks into Paul's face for signs of the bullet but finds none. Restored. All restored.

And Alex? What about Alex? Where was he?

So this was what she had held in her arms, and for this she had shed her tears, and from this she had sought escape in the embrace of Jesus, who had healed her. No, this wasn't acceptable. It was not. *At midnight, the Lord remembers.*

She was the soul in exile, a vocation whose meaning takes eons to grasp. Fortunately she had also become an American and no longer had to accept the given as final. Everything existed only in draft, to be revised over and over. She could reorder her past, reconfigure it however she wished. She could repair it. Everything could still be redeemed.

Except Alex. Her son had failed her too often. He hadn't become the savior she'd needed, the one she and the others of her generation, who suffered as they had, had counted on. He'd turned out badly, a wasted effort, an insult, a shame. She had to show him how wrong he was to have acted as he had.

So I imagine her arguing with herself, her soul a bloody shawl sticking to a thousand unstaunched wounds we in our enlightened age, in the heart of the empire of outrageous privilege, would tell her to take to a therapist or a healer—though of course she would dub such a response pagan, and would she be far from wrong? So I imagine, but even imagination has limits.

At midnight the Lord remembers the bones of the hind lying in the dust—and not only the hind. At midnight the Lord hears again every scream that ever cut through the air, reaching toward him, fearing He'd gone. At midnight, the Lord God recalls every hair that has ever fallen from the head of a shaken child. At midnight, the Lord repents of his silence, shedding two tears that turn to flames and hang in clouds of fire above the earth. The four hundred worlds shudder before the Lord's despair. And the Lord God bends over his creation and whispers. And the righteous rise up and sing: "Hear the voice over the waters! Praise be Thou, who revealest Thy secret to those who fear Thee, He who knoweth the mysteries." And the angels appear in visions to the righteous of the world, explaining that God's silence must not be confused with indifference. So Ada hears the words and knows at last that her losses were purposeful, though it remains up to her to enact the meaning of her grief, and thereby to end it.